YJ

ETERNAL SEAS

"A thrilling and magical adventure with plenty of hair-raising chases and a villain readers will love to hate. ETERNAL SEAS is a must-read for young fantasy fans."

Madeline Dyer, author of the *Untamed* series

"ETERNAL SEAS is a compelling adventure that weaves mystery and intrigue into a tantalising plot for the reader to enjoy. The writing has a lyrical quality and almost seems to capture the movement of the sea as the story unfolds. A very enjoyable read."

Jude Lennon, author of *Hal and the End Street*, the *Lamby* series and other children's books

"An exciting debut novel by Lexi Rees that takes us on a roller coaster adventure ride over high seas to mysterious places and brims with magic and intrigue. Young readers will love this book."

Shalbey Bellaman, author of *Dragons in the Looking Glass* and *Jack in the Wallows*

ETERNAL SEAS

LEXI REES

Matador
9 Priory Business Park,
Wistow Road, Kibworth Beauchamp,
Leicestershire. LE8 0RX
Tel: 0116 279 2299
Email: books@troubador.co.uk
Web: www.troubador.co.uk/matador
Twitter: @matadorbooks

ISBN 978 1789014 648

British Library Cataloguing in Publication Data.
A catalogue record for this book is available from the British Library.

Printed and bound by CPI Group (UK) Ltd, Croydon, CR0 4YY
Typeset in 12pt Aldine401 BT by Troubador Publishing Ltd, Leicester, UK

Matador is an imprint of Troubador Publishing Ltd

MIX
Paper from
responsible sources
FSC
www.fsc.org   FSC® C013604

For Finlay,
my inspiration.

"Difficulties are just things
to overcome, after all."

Ernest Shackleton, explorer, 1874 – 1922

PROLOGUE

Defeated by the Earth Lords during the Last War, the other clans were forced deep into hiding, locking away their powers in mysterious relics.

As the centuries passed, people forgot these powers ever existed. They faded into myths and legends, bedtime stories for children about magical people who could control the waves and walk amongst the clouds.

Today we go about our daily lives, unaware of how ordinary we have become.

But not everyone forgot.

The guardians, who protect the relics, did not forget.

The clan elders, who wait patiently, did not forget.

And Sir Waldred, the ruthless leader of the Earth Lords, will never forget. He will not stop until the relics are found … and destroyed. Only then will his reign be unchallenged. Forever.

We didn't know it that morning, but our lives were about to become much less ordinary, and a lot more dangerous.

ONE

SMUGGLERS

My lungs cry for air.

'How long was I down there?'

My sister, Aria, checks her watch. 'That was almost eleven minutes, Finn. You're weird. Nobody can hold their breath that long.'

'That's my best ever,' I say.

I splash around in the gentle waves, relishing the push and pull of the tide against my skin, the water as warm as a bath.

'I reckon I can do even longer … time me again.' Without waiting for a reply, I sink.

Her muffled voice filters through the water. 'Wave at me or something this time so I know you're OK.'

Determined to break fifteen minutes, I settle cross-legged at the bottom of the sea like a Buddhist monk. One minute … two minutes … five minutes. Time slides past.

I roll over onto the sandy seabed. Tiny, translucent crabs chase each other round a pile of rocks.

'Hello,' I say, prodding one and forcing it to stop. 'What are you doing?'

'Run round rock.'

'But why?'

'Must run. Everyone running,' it says, panting. 'Running from something. Running to something. Don't matter, still running.'

'I'm not running.'

'Course you running! Maybe you not know yet, but the sea knows. The sea watches you. The sea fears for you.'

'What do you mean?' I ask, but he's wriggled free and scuttled off down a hole. Something brushes lightly against my foot. A luminous fish nibbles my big toe. It tickles. I laugh, and it darts away.

The dark curve of the hull of our home, a boat called the *Alcina*, floats several metres above me. Aria's wobbly outline shimmers in the ripples as she hangs over the polished wood railing on the side of the boat. Her long white hair flutters in the wind. She looks so like Mum, I choke back a sob. She waves wildly at me. Something's wrong. I push off and swim upwards.

The instant my head's above the water, she starts to babble, 'Hurry up, Finn, get on board.' Muttered complaints of, 'Why is he still in the water?' and,

'Why doesn't he ever help?' reach me.

I clamber up the ladder onto the boat. Water droplets fly off in all directions as I shake my head.

Aria dashes past, stowing away snorkels, masks, flippers, towels, and sunscreen; all the loose items that seem to accumulate on deck when you're at anchor. She's still grumbling.

'Hey, that's not fair!' I protest, clearing the water out of my ears. 'I'm out now. Anyway, why are we in such a rush all of a sudden? What's going on?'

'Dad's got to pick up a parcel. He's almost ready to lift the anchor. Come on, slow coach,' she says, grabbing my arm and dragging me along behind her.

Dad's waiting at the wheel. His white hair tucked under a baseball cap and his shirt sleeves rolled up, exposing pale forearms. Despite spending all day outdoors, he never seems to tan.

The windlass groans as it yanks the anchor loose and then we're free. The *Alcina* skips and dances as we turn into the wind to raise the main sail. I cartwheel across the deck, landing as lightly as a cat. Aria glowers at me, her hands on her hips.

Dad sets the course and leaves us at the helm.

'Aria, did Dad say anything about the pick-up?' I ask, studying the compass.

'No, nothing at all,' she says, tapping the glass. The compass needle wobbles, but then settles back where it was.

East.
We stare at it for a while.
Still east.
'Dad, why are we going east?' Aria calls. 'Are we not doing the usual route?'

'No, not this time. We've got a new route. The pickup location is in Izmarli,' Dad says, busying himself with a pile of charts.

'Izmarli?' I ask. 'But you swore you'd never set foot on that island. You said it's full of trackers and bounty hunters.'

'It is. Zooming around on their jet-ships and motorbikes, terrorising the locals. Pretending to help the authorities catch criminals when it's them that are the real trouble makers …' Dad thumps the chart table.

'Do we really have to go there?' Aria asks. 'What if they catch us?'

'Yes, we do. Don't worry though. They won't catch us. Nobody knows these routes as well as we do,' Dad says with a tight lipped smile.

Sunlight bounces off the compass, illuminating the silver needle. Then it hits me ... he's wrong. This is *not* a route we know: those routes are far enough off the beaten track to keep us safe, and familiar enough that we know every hiding spot. This new route is dangerous. I open my mouth to argue, but Dad glares at me and jerks his thumb in Aria's direction. I close it again.

'So, once we pick up the parcel from Izmarli, where's the delivery?' Aria asks, apparently reassured by Dad's comment about the route.

'New London.'

'N-N-New L-London?' Aria stammers. Enclosed by the high stone city walls since the Last War, strangers are forbidden to enter. 'Dad, you know how much they hate strangers, especially smugglers. Why would you take us there?'

'It's a job,' Dad says.

'Do we need the money?' I ask, frowning.

'It's a bit more complicated than that, Finn. One day you'll understand. I have no choice,' he says, turning his back on us and fiddling with the sails.

Aria and I sit in silence. She twists a chunk of hair into a tight ringlet and chews the end. After a while, she turns to me. 'I don't get it. Why's Dad taking us to New London? It's too dangerous. It's not worth the risk.'

'I'm sure it'll be fine. Dad will have it all worked out.' I put my arm around her shoulders. 'Hey, your muscles are getting big! Where have you put my skinny little sister?'

'Haha,' she says, punching me playfully. 'You should do more work on the boat if you want muscles.' She lets go of the twisted strand and it drops back into the smooth white curtain of hair. 'Bet I could beat you at an arm wrestle now.' She holds her arm up in challenge.

'Challenge accepted. On the count of three. Ready? One … two …'

She smashes my hand onto the deck.

'You cheated. I didn't say *three*. I wasn't ready,' I protest. 'Let's go again.'

'No chance.'

She lies back on the deck, smirking. I flop down next her. Thin white clouds scurry across the sky, dragged by the wind on an unknown journey.

Aria pushes herself upright. 'I don't like this route. I'm scared.'

'Look, don't worry. I reckon he's been planning this for ages. You know how he's been buried in his cabin for weeks, this is what he must have been organising.'

'Suppose so,' she says. 'At least we can look for

Mum when we're in Izmarli. Maybe someone will have seen her.'

Mum's absence cuts me as cold and sharp today as it did on the day she disappeared but I bundle up the emotion and lock it away.

'Aria, she's gone,' I say. 'We don't know if she's dead or alive. Even if she *is* alive, I don't think she wants to be found. You have to let her go.'

'She's not dead. I'd know.'

'Aria …'

She springs to her feet, her eyes blazing. 'Shut up. You don't understand. You don't care about anyone except yourself. I'll never stop looking for her. Not while there's a chance she's still alive.' She turns on her heel and storms off, slamming the cabin door behind her.

I sit on deck alone, thinking about Mum, while the sun slides towards the horizon. The hours pass and the waves of pain retreat into the gaping hole in my heart.

Aria hasn't come out of her cabin. I haul myself upright and tap on her door. 'Aria, I'm sorry.'

Silence.

'Can I come in?'

'Go away.'

'I know you're mad at me, but I really am sorry. I miss her too. Please can I come in?'

'I don't want to talk to you. I won't give up on Mum. She wouldn't give up on us.'

'I know. You're right. I'll help you look for her in Izmarli.'

'I don't need your help, Finn. I'll find her myself.'

'I'm going to help anyway,' I say to the door. 'Please let me in …'

Nothing.

I try a different topic. 'I wanted to ask you about the parcel …'

The door opens a crack, curiosity defeating the sulk.

'It must be a very special job,' she says, sticking her head out. Her hair is all mussed up and her eyes are red and puffy.

She opens the door wider and lets me inside her long, narrow cabin. A brightly painted mural runs along one wall: giant eagles and gliding albatross, colourful hummingbirds and cheerful robins, strutting crows and swooping seagulls, mythical dodos and sea-green scaled dragons. Everything else in the room is pure white: white wooden floorboards, white bedspread, white cushions.

'Do you think the parcel might be gold?' I ask.

'No. I don't think so,' she says. 'Dad won't take the risk of carrying gold anymore. The pirates can track it too easily. They'd attack us, and we don't have any weapons on board.' She laughs, 'Your penknife doesn't count.'

'It does,' I joke back, 'but your bow and arrow doesn't.' I pull a face at her and scramble out of reach. She chases after me, shrieking. We sprint up onto the deck, scampering up and down the rigging in a three-dimensional game of tag until we collapse, panting.

But that night, the parcel haunts my dreams. *What could it be? What could be so important that Dad would put us in such danger?*

CHALLENGE

The voyage passes quietly. Small islands stud the sea along the route; soil and tree trunks blending together into a rusty orange colour. Thirsty-looking, silvery-green leaves dot the tree branches. Stony beaches line the tiny bays where we anchor at night.

Each morning, after breakfast, we pull up the anchor and set sail. East and further east. The winds hold steady. Despite the danger, I'm looking forward to visiting Izmarli.

I finish another book and cram it onto a shelf. Stretching out on my bed, I look around my cabin. It's an odd shape, tucked into the bow of the boat, tapering gently to a point. Light streams through the portholes, landing in golden circles on the wooden walls. The mottled green leather top of a battered desk is just visible under piles of books, papers and trinkets. Clothes tumble onto the floor from partially open drawers, their brass handles dulled with age. My favourite painting hangs lopsidedly above my bed.

With a burst of activity, I sit up, swing my legs off the bed and crawl underneath. Somewhere, amongst the tatty trainers, odd socks and discarded toys, is a stash of unread books. While I'm searching through the mess, a muffled cry from the deck reaches me, 'Land ahoy.'

I wriggle backwards out of the hole and race up on deck to look, beating Aria by a few seconds. Dense jungle encircles a vast mountain. A huge waterfall cascades down one side of the mountain.

'That's the weirdest looking island I've ever seen,' I say. 'Where's the harbour?'

'It's through there.' Dad points at a narrow slit in the rocks.

Inside, it opens into another world. A bustling port wraps around the wide bay, almost tumbling over the harbour walls and into the sea in its enthusiasm for life.

We pick our way through the jumble of old wooden boats, their once bright paint faded and flaking. Fishing nets and lobster pots lie in reeking piles, the pungent aroma of rotten fish wafting off them. Scruffy dogs run loose. Stray cats sunbathe on the rocks, waiting lazily for the fishermen to throw them scraps. Aria will no doubt feed them later.

'Can I helm this time, please Dad?' Aria asks.

'No, you're better at handling the ropes,' Dad says firmly.

Aria pulls a face at me and stomps off.

'Astern,' Dad yells.

I spin the dark wooden wheel. Despite the size of the boat, she's easy to manoeuvre.

A crowd of locals and tourists gather to watch us. Shopkeepers jostle each other, holding up wicker baskets overflowing with fresh fruit and vegetables. Grown-ups with sunburnt faces sweat in the heat. Street urchins try to pilfer sweets and toys from the market stalls. The whole mob seems to crave some drama to break up the day. Falling in the water whilst trying to jump ashore would result in peals of laughter. Crashing into another boat would draw cries of 'oooh' and 'aaah'. Even just a lot of shouting would make them smile.

Aria leaps off the boat and onto the quay. She heaves on our mooring lines and secures them to the rusty iron rings on the harbour wall. We've done this a gazillion times and our routine is slick, choreographed to precision through years of practice. It's not long before we're safely tied up against the harbour wall. In the absence of any drama, the crowd loses interest and drifts off.

On shore, Aria stands with her feet planted apart, hands on her hips. She breathes in deeply. 'I do like sailing, well except when I get seasick, but honestly nothing beats those first few steps ashore after a long trip.'

'Got to disagree there, Aria,' I say. 'I could happily live on the sea and never set foot on land.'

She pulls a face at me.

'Dad, can we get honey ice?' I ask, my tongue tingling. There's no freezer on the boat so it's a luxury. Mum used to buy them for us as a treat. Even though she's gone, it's still part of the ritual when we arrive in port.

Dad laughs. 'There I was thinking you'd forgotten. Here, go and see if they have any.' He passes us a few coins and smiles. 'But stay close to the boat. And don't go into the bazaar. I'm going to get the parcel.'

With that, he strides off into the grand bazaar. His white hair glows like a beacon in the sea of dark-haired heads, until it's finally swallowed up by the crowds.

A few minutes later we're sitting on the harbour wall, our feet dangling above the water, honey ice half-eaten and melting fast.

A group of local kids gathers around us, babbling happily in a language I don't understand. A few of the braver kids practise their English, the unfamiliar sounds getting tangled in their mouths. 'Where you are from?', 'What your name is?', 'How many years have you?' The usual questions. 'My brother bigger than you.' The usual taunts.

'I bet I'm stronger than him,' I say to the kid with the big brother. Aria jabs me hard in the ribs with her elbow.

'He biggest boy in town.'

'Can he swim?' I ask. Aria glares at me and kicks me on the shin.

'He best swimmer in world,' says the kid, his chest jutting forward. 'I get him. He prove.' He skips off into the crowd.

'Don't do this,' Aria hisses. 'You'll get us in trouble again.'

The kid reappears, a youth strutting beside him.

'Hey,' I say.

'Hey,' says the youth, crossing his arms.

'Swim! Swim! Swim!' the kid cries, bouncing up and down with excitement. The other kids pick up the chant and join in.

I slurp the last of my honey ice, lick my fingers, and slide off the harbour wall into the water.

The youth kicks off his sandals and dives in after me.

I challenge him, 'How long can you hold your breath for?'

'Longer than you, I bet,' he says, clamping his nose shut and sinking into the sea.

After a few minutes, he claws his way back to the surface, gulping the air hungrily. I bob up a few seconds later and pretend to pant a few times so it looks convincing. 'Good effort,' I say.

The boy hauls himself out of the water and ambles back to his mates. The gang drifts away, laughing and shoving each other playfully.

There's still no sign of Dad. I scuff my feet on the ground and stoop to pick up a smooth flat stone. I skim it over the water, counting seven bounces before it sinks.

'I'm bored,' I moan. 'Let's explore.'

'We can't. We promised Dad we'd stay close to the boat. It's too dangerous here,' Aria says. But it's too late. She's talking to the back of my head. I've ducked into the bazaar.

THREE

LOST

I pluck a ripe fruit from a nearby stall and drop a silver coin into the honesty jar. I casually toss the fruit in the air and catch it a few times before taking a huge bite.

Aria catches up with me.

We wander around the market stalls. The casual buzz of daily life cocoons us, drawing us in. Soon the rabbit warren of twisting alleys swallows us and we're quickly out of sight of the boat. Deeper and deeper into the maze we go. The stalls get closer together, until there's virtually no natural light. The cheerful chatter dies, replaced with a leaden echo. I slow down. Aria clutches my arm tightly. Ahead, a dead end looms.

Aria starts to turn and retrace our steps but, right at the furthest point, I spy a stall selling the weirdest collection of objects I've ever seen: walrus teeth with intricate ink sketches on them, pebbles covered in an ancient script that I can't read, knotted string and feather dream-catchers, bronze amulets. I drag the reluctant Aria towards it.

The stall-keeper glares at me. His piercing blue eyes seem to slice though my skull and into my thoughts. I try to hold his stare, but it's too intense. I wither before him, shrinking into insignificance.

'You should not be here,' he growls, his voice dark and menacing. 'It is not safe.'

I pluck up the courage to ask him a question, 'Do you have a pirrfu sea-charm, please, in dime gold?' My voice comes out strangely high pitched and squeaky. 'I've been looking for one to add to my collection for ages and this seems just the kind of stall to sell them.'

'Even if I did, I wouldn't sell it to you,' he snaps. I knew customer service wasn't going to be his strong point. 'You don't know how to use it. You have neither the talent nor the training.'

What? Why would I need talent or training? It's just a trinket for my collection. It's not as if it could be a magical pirrfu charm. They don't exist. They're just stories. Surely, he doesn't think his charms are real? Mad old man. Of course, I don't say that. Instead I mumble, 'Errrr … I'll find a teacher.'

'What teacher would want you,' he snorts.

I shuffle my feet uncomfortably.

He rubs his nose. 'Yet, I sense it calls to you.' He rummages below the counter, grunting and

 grumbling. He stands up and glowers at me, then uncurls a gnarled hand to reveal the most beautiful charm I've ever seen. Spiralling, like an ammonite shell, the design flows into a wave shape. Even in the weak light of the market, the dime gold glows subtly, a stark contrast to the filthy stall.

'It's beautiful,' I say, my fingers itching to stroke it. 'Is that pure dime gold? It can't be …' My voice trails off.

He snatches it away. 'It's 723 crowns. If you are ready.'

I convert that into pounds. 'That's outrageous. My other charms cost only a fraction of that.'

The stall-keeper shrugs and stashes the charm back under the counter.

'Wait,' I cry. 'Maybe …'

Dad emerges from the shadows, 'What are you two doing here?' he snaps. 'I told you to stay near the boat. It's not safe here.'

That's the second time in two minutes someone has said it's not safe here. Suddenly, I long to be back at the waterfront, standing in the daylight, feeling a gentle breeze, breathing the salty air. Not here in the depths of this sweltering, sticky bazaar, bombarded by pungent aromas and clamouring noise.

While Dad's not looking, I slide all my savings into the stall-keeper's hand. There's no time to haggle.

He presses the charm into my palm and wraps my fingers around it. He mumbles a few words, a curse or a protective charm. It's too late to worry though. Whatever they were, once spoken, they cannot be unspoken.

'This pirrfu charm is the mark of a Sea-Tamer,' he says aloud. 'Danger will follow you. The teacher you need is at the Castle. They will decide if you are ready. It is not my path. Another must guide you.'

Before I can ask what he means, Dad ushers us away from the curious stall and marches through the maze. I glance back but it has faded into the darkness, as if it never existed.

Dad navigates the maze of stalls with confidence. I get the distinct feeling he knows the way. Clearly this is not his first visit to Izmarli. I clutch the charm tightly in my palm. It pulses, beating like a heart, softly at first, but then harder and faster. I open my hand and stare at it. The pulsing stops. *Did I imagine it?*

As the stalls thin out and the sunlight reappears, I start to relax. I brush off the fear I felt in the dark alleys at the heart of the bazaar, but the grim warning from the stall-keeper sends a shiver down my spine.

I look at Dad; his hands are empty. 'Did you get the parcel?' I ask, my eyes scanning his pockets for unusual lumps and bumps.

'Not exactly. I met them but they didn't have it with them. We have to pick it up inland.'

'Oh. That's a bit weird, isn't it? Why didn't they bring it to the port like normal?' Everything about this delivery seems to be unusual.

'Well, apparently, they haven't actually got it,' Dad starts.

'What? Have we wasted our time coming here?'

'No. I don't think so. They claim to know where it is,' he continues. 'They've given me a map, but they want me to find it. They want us to find it …' He pauses, his eyes flick towards me. 'Actually Finn, they want you to find it.'

'Me?' I stop dead in my tracks.

Dad doesn't break stride. Aria jogs to keep up with him. She tugs at his sleeve and, with a conspiratorial look, he leans over and whispers a few words in her ear. Aria gives the tiniest of nods.

I run to catch up. 'What is it? What were you two talking about then?'

'Nothing,' they chime as we emerge from the bazaar onto the quay right beside our boat.

'But …' I hop onto the boat after them.

'Finn, not now.'

'But, Dad …' He glares at me, his face stony. I might as well talk to a brick wall.

Back on the boat, we settle around the saloon table. Dad produces a piece of paper from his pocket. He flattens it out in front of us. 'This is the map they gave me. It shows where we have to go to pick up the parcel.'

We study the route, following the marked track inland to the mountain.

Dad points out of the porthole at the mountain soaring from the centre of the island. 'It's up there,' he says. 'We need to get to the bottom of that waterfall.'

Aria and I look where he's pointing and try to trace a path up the steep mountainside.

'All the way up there?' I say in horror.

The waterfall pours from a gap high in the mountainside. It lands on a plateau about half way down the barren cliff creating an oasis. From there, the river cuts a deep gully before disappearing into the jungle.

While we're still staring out of the porthole at the mountain, Dad gasps. I spin round to see what happened. He quickly folds up the map and, without warning, dashes up onto the deck, jumps ashore, and marches back into the bazaar.

'What happened there? Let's go after him,' I say, ready to follow him.

'No,' Aria says firmly. 'I think we'd better stay here and wait for him. He wasn't very happy when he found us in the middle of the bazaar earlier.'

I lean back, put my feet up on the table, and spin the pirrfu charm round and round between my fingers restlessly.

Several hours pass before Dad comes back to the boat, looking bleak. Without a word, he disappears into his cabin.

I follow him.

'What's wrong, Dad?' I ask.

'I tried to find the customer, I wanted to ask them about …' he says, his forehead creased with worry.

'Ask them about what? Is everything OK?'

'I just wanted to ask them a question.'

'And? What did they say?'

'I couldn't find them. They'd vanished. The place we met was deserted, as if they'd never been there. Nobody had seen them leave, or knew where they'd gone.'

'Oh. So what was the question you needed to ask them so badly?'

'Nothing.'

'You can tell me, Dad. I'm old enough. It's clearly not nothing. You wouldn't have rushed off like that for nothing. You saw something on the map, didn't you? What was it? You can trust me, please.'

'I'm not sure. It just surprised me … OK. Maybe you should know,' he says, digging the map out of his pocket. He points at a small scribble in the corner. It's a signature. I pull the paper towards me and read it …

Morgan.

'Who's that?' I ask.

FOUR

GONE

'It's a long story,' he says, taking a deep breath, 'but first, it's time I told you something.'

He stops and puts a shaky hand on my shoulder. 'You'd better sit down,' he says.

'OK,' I say, a wave of nerves washing over me. *Why is he being all strange?*

'This is not easy to say. Before I start, you must know that I love you with all my heart.'

Beads of sweat form on his forehead, even though the evening is cool.

'Isolda and I knew this time would come, that one day you would need to know the truth. But I always thought she would be here to tell you the story …'

'Just tell me, Dad. It's OK.'

'Finn, there's no easy way to say this. I don't know where to start.'

He stops, wipes his brow and takes a deep breath.

'It's about you, your birth. Your mother and I are not your birth parents. When you were born, it wasn't possible for you to stay with them, so Isolda and I offered to look after you. We were so happy to have you join our family. We've tried to tell you many times, but we just didn't know how.'

I'm adopted. How could I not have known? My hand flies up to my mouth, I'm confused. I break out in a cold sweat, and my heart beats so fast I think it's going to burst. I take a deep breath and count to ten. It doesn't help. A million questions zoom round my head, making me feel dizzy, and I fire them at Dad.

'Who are my birth parents? Are they alive?'

'They're alive. They're called Kallan and Morgan.'

'What are they like?'

'They were great friends of ours. Always fun to be with. Talented and clever too.'

'Do I look like them?' I'd always been aware I looked different with my tousled mop of dark brown curly hair and deeply tanned skin, but never really given it any thought.

'Yes. The older you get, the more you look like Kallan.'

'Aria's not adopted, is she?'

'No, she's your step-sister.'

'That makes sense,' I say. 'When did you last see Kallan and Morgan? Where are they now?'

'I'm sorry, I haven't seen them in years, I don't even know where they are. It was difficult to keep in touch.'

I sink into silence, trying to make sense of all this.

'You said I couldn't stay with them. Why couldn't I stay with them?' The words stick in my throat.

'Kallan and Morgan had no choice. They didn't want to give you up, but it was too dangerous for you to stay with them. This was the only way they could protect you. After you'd gone, they struggled with the loss. They were both very sad. Kallan buried himself in his work, but Morgan never really recovered.'

'But why would they agree to give me up if it hurt them both so badly?'

'They were forced to.'

'By whom?'

'The clan elders. Neither of them were OK about it. It hurt them both, but Kallan understood the clan perspective better. Morgan didn't. She begged them to find another way, but there wasn't any option. She argued with them, but your safety was the priority for the clan. Afterwards, she blamed the elders for forcing her to give you away, even though she knew it was the only way to keep you safe.'

'Safe from what though?' I can barely breathe.

'You know the legends about the old clan magic?'

'Yes, Mum used to tell us about them. Magic from the earth, fire, air and water. But they were just myths.'

'Not myths, no. Once there was magic everywhere. Now, it's virtually gone. Very occasionally, a child is born with the clan magic in their blood.'

'And I'm one of those children,' I interrupt, suddenly grasping who I am. 'That's why I can talk to the sea creatures, and why I can stay under water for so long.'

'Exactly. You're one of those children. You're a Sea-Tamer. When you're older, I reckon you'll be a powerful one. I know you can feel some of your powers already, but you haven't even begun to realise how much you can do.'

'Are there others like me? Blood-magic children?'

'Yes. There are several others hidden around the world. They're all younger than you though, and still waiting for their full powers to come through. Ar ...' He stops and frowns. The word hangs unfinished.

'How many of us are there?'

'One from each clan. Legend says that, together, you have the power to restore magic to the world. But if Sir Waldred finds you, he'll kill you. That's why Kallan and Morgan had to hide you.'

'Sir Waldred?' The name makes me shudder. Every child has heard tales about the ruthless Earth Lord. Life is usually easier, and longer, if *he* doesn't hear tales about *you* though.

'He's murdered other blood-magic children before you. The ones the elders failed to protect. You're the first to live long enough to get your full powers.'

'He murdered them? Why would he do that? To stop the prophecy coming true? To stop magic being returned to the world? Surely having magic back would be a good thing?'

'Not for him it wouldn't. If magic returns, Sir Waldred will no longer be the most powerful Lord in the world. He'll do anything to prevent magic being restored. Murder is nothing.'

The choice my birth parents made makes sense. I now understand why they had to give me away to keep me safe.

'What about the other blood-magic children?' I ask.

'The elders hope they will survive long enough to come into their powers too.'

'I hope so too. So how did I end up with you?'

'You needed to vanish from sight, and that's exactly what smugglers do: we're invisible.' Dad puts his arm around me and holds me tight. 'I know it's a lot to take in, but we're still your family.'

'It's OK, Dad, I know you are,' I say. 'You've always been around for me. Nothing has changed. Nothing could ever change that. But it must have been very hard for Kallan and Morgan.'

'It was.'

'Would you mind if I wanted to meet them?'

'I don't know if it's possible, but if that's what you want then yes, of course I'll help you look for them.'

I pull the map towards me and point at the scribble. 'Do you think this might help us find them? Are you sure this is her signature? After all, Morgan is not an unusual name.'

'Yes,' Dad says. 'It's definitely her signature. Look at it closely.'

I run my finger underneath it, stopping at the letter "o" of Morgan. It's been replaced by a symbol. A pirffu charm.

'She always used that symbol in her signature. She was proud to be a Sea-Tamer.'

'Is she here, in Izmarli?'

'No, she didn't give me the map. I promise, I'd tell you if she was here.'

'Even if she didn't give it to you directly, it's still a clue. The customer must know her. Morgan drew the map for them. If we find them, then they can help us find her.'

'Finn, trust me, they're long gone. I told you, that's what I was doing earlier. As soon as I spotted her signature, I went back to the market to look for them, but I couldn't find them anywhere. They'd literally vanished without a trace.'

'But you must know who the customer is?'

'You know how smugglers work: *"Don't ask questions and you won't be told lies"*, so no, I don't know who the customer is. They were … strange. Even more secretive than usual. I never got a name.'

'Oh. Maybe we can still work out who they are. What did they look like?'

'Whoever gave me the map was covered from head to toe by a thick woollen cloak, I remember thinking they must be melting in this heat. It had a large hood which fell over their face. I didn't even get a glimpse of them.'

'It's impossible,' I sigh, scratching my head. 'Perhaps the people we're delivering it to can help us? We can ask them when we give it to them.'

'It's not that simple. They might not want to tell us anything, Finn. Don't get your hopes up.'

'We have to try though, Dad. Come on, let's go and get the parcel.' I'm on my feet, itching to go.

'Not tonight, Finn,' Dad says. 'It's late, and we need to be properly prepared. We'll chat about it tomorrow with Aria. Get some sleep, tomorrow's going to be a long day.'

I start to protest but he folds up the map and puts it away.

Tossing and turning in bed, I think through the conversation – my adoption, my clan powers, the other blood-magic children, the prophecy, Sir

Waldred, the map, Morgan's signature. Eventually my eyelids get heavy and I nod off into a restless sleep.

Despite my world being turned upside down, the sun rises the next day, bright and optimistic. I pull on the same clothes as yesterday and tiptoe past Aria's door, trying not to wake her up. I creep into Dad's cabin and close the door, wincing at the loud creak.

'Dad,' I whisper, shaking him gently to wake him up.

He yawns, stretching like a cat.

'Morning,' he says, groggily.

'Does Aria know I'm a Sea-Tamer? Does she know about Kallan and Morgan?'

'No. We thought it should be your decision when you wanted to tell her.'

'I think we should tell her today.'

'OK, after breakfast. Do you want to tell her yourself, or with me?'

'On my own, I think. Is that OK?'

'Yes, it's your decision.'

'Thanks. Another question was bugging me during the night, Dad. Why is Morgan involved with this parcel? It's connected to the elders, isn't it?' I ask.

He sits bolt upright.

'I was worrying about that too, Finn,' Dad says. 'I think it might be. She never forgave the elders for taking you away from her. She swore to take revenge on them. If she's involved, this parcel is even more dangerous than I thought.'

I look at Dad, his brow furrowed and his eyes full of fear. *What secrets lie within this parcel?* My stomach twists into a tight knot.

My heart skips a beat. For this delivery, we won't just be avoiding the usual pirates. We're caught in a tangled web between Morgan, the elders, and a mysterious customer.

'I'm going to tell Aria now. She needs to know the danger too,' I say.

'OK. Go and wake her up. Let me know when you want me to join you,' Dad says, sinking back onto the mattress and pulling the covers up.

Over breakfast, I tell Aria who I really am.

'I wondered,' she says with a grin. 'That's so cool. I knew holding your breath that long wasn't normal.' She bites her lip. 'Did Dad say anything about me?'

'No. Just that he hadn't told you about me. He said it was up to me to tell you.'

'Oh,' she says, sounding a bit disappointed. 'I wondered if he'd said anything else.'

'He told me he was trying to find the customer when he dashed back into the bazaar. Look at this,' I say, pointing at the signature on the map. 'Dad is sure this is my birth mother's signature. He says it makes the delivery more dangerous.'

'It's curious,' she says. 'I wonder how it's all connected.'

'I don't know. Something doesn't feel right. I don't think Dad has told us everything.'

FIVE

MISTAKE

Breakfast is cleared away by the time Dad comes in. 'We'd better get going,' he says. 'Take a small backpack with anything you need. We'll probably have to camp overnight.'

I gaze around absent-mindedly and decide I don't want to carry anything. I shove my feet into my battered walking boots and slip my penknife into my pocket.

Aria rushes about, gathering a rapidly expanding pile of kit. 'You could help me sort out the stuff,' she says.

'What else do we need? I'm ready.'

'You're not ready; you don't even have a backpack,' she retorts.

Despite the messiness of the boat, she quickly locates three sleeping mats, some dried fruit and nuts, and our water bottles. She picks up the fire starter kit with its flint stick and a battered tin of silver birch bark shavings, then slings her bow and arrow over her shoulder. As I start to get off the boat, she blocks my way, holding out an overflowing backpack. 'If you think I'm carrying this for you, you're wrong,' she says.

We set off through the jungle towards the mountain. Thick vegetation slows our progress. We hack our way through the dense tangle of undergrowth. Sweat streams down my back and my T-shirt clings uncomfortably to my body. There's still a long way to go and my legs ache.

Gradually the vegetation starts to thin. The ground gets steeper and rockier. In several places, we scramble on hands and knees. It isn't long before my arms and legs are covered in scratches. Eventually, we emerge from the trees altogether and get a clear view down to the harbour.

'Look how small our boat is. I can't believe

we've climbed so far already,' Aria exclaims.

From here, a narrow path is hewn into the rock face. It zig-zags relentlessly up the side of the mountain. In places, the path is little more than a ledge, forcing us to shuffle sideways, barely daring to breathe, until it widens again.

Every so often we pass a hollow, hacked into the rock face. Ancient burial tombs, Dad explains.

I stumble on a patch of loose gravel. Stones scurry over the edge of the cliff. I land on my stomach and start sliding down the steep path, faster and faster. The grit stings my skin as I scratch and claw at it, trying to find something solid to clasp onto. Blood pours from my fingers, my t-shirt rips into shreds. I dig my toes into the ground as hard as I can, thankful for the protection of my walking boots. It's not enough.

The path turns a sharp corner but momentum carries my body straight on, towards the edge of the cliff. Like when you're on a roller coaster, even though you know you're about to plunge down, I'm helpless. I can't stop. I'm feel myself going over. My feet thrash wildly in the fresh air, failing to find a foothold.

My fingertips close around a branch. I cling onto it desperately. *Will it hold my weight?* Inch by inch, I grind to a halt, my legs swinging over the ledge. I hold my breath, count to three, then look up.

It's not a branch that saved my life. It's Aria's

bow. Her arm is hooked around a rock, her face a mask of concentration, straining against my weight dangling off the other end of her bow. 'Hold on,' she yells at me, bracing herself against the rock.

Dad throws himself onto the ground, spread-eagled, and grabs my other hand. He drags me back over the ledge, rocks scraping against my stomach. The three of us collapse into a heap on the ground, breathing fast and hard. Aria hugs her bow to her chest.

I stand up, wincing, and examine my cuts and bruises. I'll have a few scars, but no permanent damage. 'That was a close shave,' I say.

Dad pulls himself to his feet. He wipes the blood off the deepest cut on my leg and frowns. 'Can you walk? We need to keep going.'

'I'm OK,' I say.

We start to climb again. I try not to limp. Each of us walks a little more slowly, and much more carefully.

Dad stops in front of one of the man-made caves and looks around. This one is big enough for the three of us to crawl inside.

'I don't think we should try and go any further today. It's getting dark,' Dad says. 'Let's set up camp here for the night.'

'It's creepy,' Aria moans.

'The spirit of whoever was buried here will protect us. It's actually probably the safest place we could be,' Dad says.

Camp is basic. We unroll our sleeping mats. Strange noises echo in the jungle below us, and an ominous silence presses down from the mountain above. The rocky ground makes a hard bed. With the setting sun, the temperature plummets, but there's nothing to build a fire with. Cold and uncomfortable, I sleep little and we're all up at dawn.

Breakfast is a handful of berries and some of the nuts that Aria had sensibly packed. Gathering up our kit doesn't take long and we're soon on our way.

Then we're climbing again, following the path as it snakes its way up the steep mountain. After a few hours, I'm tempted to ask if we are nearly there yet. It's a pointless question as Dad will reply, 'Just round the next corner'. But it seems that there is no end to the corners; after each zig, there is a zag, and we just keep on going up and up and up.

We walk all day, stopping only briefly to rest and take a few sips of water. It's late by the time we reach the flat plateau at the bottom of the waterfall that we could see from the boat. Up close, it's even bigger, cascading from a dizzying height into an inky black pool. The water roars like a lion as it crashes into the pool and we shout at each other over the noise. Trees crowd around the pool, like an oasis in a rocky desert.

As I get closer to the pool, my head fills with a chattering noise. I can't make out the words, but I know it's fish in the pool talking to each other. I stop at the water's edge and, in my head, I shape the words, 'May I join you?'

'Yes, yes,' the fish call out to me. Freshwater fish with an unfamiliar dialect, but I can understand enough.

'Come and join us. The water is good,' one calls.

'Are you from the sea?' asks another. 'Your accent is funny.'

'Yes, I'm from the sea,' I say. 'And my accent isn't funny. It's just different.'

'What does the sea taste like?' asks the curious fish.

'Err, salty. I guess. I don't really drink it.'

Still fully clothed, I dive into the cool, refreshing water to join the chatty freshwater fish.

'No, Finn,' Dad cries.

Aria shouts, 'It might be dangerous. You don't know what's below the surface. There could be crocodiles or water snakes or anything.'

I stick my head out of the pool. 'It's OK, I did check. The fish told me it was safe,' I shout back. It's a relief being able to talk about my abilities without worrying if they'll think I'm weird or insane.

I leap up onto the rocks beside the pool. 'So, Dad, where's this pickup place then?'

'I don't know,' he admits. 'It's marked right here on the map. But it doesn't make sense. There's nothing here. I'm going to look around.'

'What are we looking for?' Aria asks.

'Anything that could hide a parcel, like a box or a chest,' Dad says.

Aria and Dad set off in different directions. The waterfall glitters and sparkles. In a trance, I walk towards it, sucked in by an invisible force.

'Finn, stop mucking about in the waterfall and help us look,' Aria calls.

I blink. The spell breaks. I edge my way back out of the waterfall but the rocks are wet and I haven't regained full control of my body from the dream-like trance. I stumble, plunging headfirst into the waterfall.

SIX

HIDDEN

I shut my eyes and wait for the force of the waterfall to drag me down into the inky pool. With a bump, I stop falling. A bump, not a splash. My eyes ping open. It's dark and damp, but I'm not underwater.

I sit up, clutching the pirrfu charm which dangles from a leather thong around my neck. It seems to be throbbing like a beating heart. With a frown, I tuck the charm back under my shirt. I look around, confused. I'm not at the bottom of the pool. Dim green light filters through a curtain of water.

'Dad? Can you hear me?' I shout. 'I'm OK. I'm in some sort of cave. Behind the waterfall.'

A few moments later Dad's head appears through the wall of water, swiftly followed by the rest of his body.

'A hidden cave. I think you've accidentally found the pickup location,' he says, raising an eyebrow.

The cascade of water at the side of the cave isn't as heavy. We step back out through the watery door and onto the rocky ledge. Pointing and waving, I yell, 'Aria! Over here.'

She jogs back towards the pool. As she gets nearer, I shout, 'There's a hidden cave. Exactly where the map shows the pickup location, we just didn't see it behind the waterfall. Hurry up. We're going in.'

'Wait for me,' she cries, her voice drowned out by the roaring waterfall as I duck back into the cave.

Shortly after, Aria emerges through the waterfall and joins me. Together, we edge our way deeper into the cave. Dad is a shadow in the gloomy darkness ahead. I wish I had a torch.

As my eyes adjust to the eerie greenish light, I look around. The cave seems to be empty, but my senses are on edge. The steady ba-dum … ba-dum … ba-dum heartbeat from the pirrfu charm accelerates. Badumbadumbadum.

A continual rumble of thunder echoes from the waterfall. Over the din, a voice calls out. Faint at first but growing louder.

'Can you hear that?' I whisper to Aria.

'Hear what?'

'That voice.'

'Nope. I can't hear anything other than the waterfall. Maybe you're imagining it.'

'I'm not. There *IS* a voice. But I can't make out what it's saying. It's kind of muffled … "See". It sounds like it's telling me to see something.'

Aria stands motionless and cups her ear, but after a few moments she shakes her head.

'I think it's coming from over there,' I say.

The voice draws me deeper into the cave, my feet moving despite the alarm bells ringing in my head. Aria follows, right on my heels. With every step, the voice gets louder and more persistent. I feel it tugging at me, pulling me closer. The darkness of the cave envelops us. I test the air in front of me with my fingertips as if in a game of blind man's bluff.

Pain sears through me. 'Ouch!' I cry, ripping my shirt open and tearing the leather thong from round my neck. A red, raw welt throbs on my chest.

'What happened?' Aria asks.

'It burnt me. My pirrfu charm. Look, it's scalding hot …' I hold it at arm's length. In the darkness, it gives off a blue glow, illuminating a solid wall. We've made it to the back of the cave. I run my hands over the surface, using the light from the charm to cut through the gloom.

'Now what are you doing?' Aria asks.

'It's here. The voice is coming from inside the rocks.'

'That's impossible.'

'I know,' I say, 'but it is.'

The walls of the cave are cold and damp. A thin film of icy water makes them slimy. Numbness spreads through my fingers and I want to give up, but the voice keeps calling to me. Finally, I feel a change in the surface.

A rough hole has been hacked into the cave wall. I peer inside, but it's too dark to see anything. I hold the charm in front of the hollow. Curious shadows dance on the rough stone under the blue light. Caught in the glow, I spot something, jammed hard into a crevice. I reach in, very slowly.

My fingertips brush against an object.

The voice screams at me. 'SEE, SEE, SEE.'

I grip the object and try to lift it from its hiding place. It's stuck. I use my fingernails to prise it out. The voice disappears. Ba-dum … ba-dum … ba-dum … A wave of calm flows from the pirrfu charm.

I open my fist and look at the parcel. It's nothing more than a small bundle wrapped in an ancient cloth; tattered, filthy and damp. It certainly doesn't look very valuable to me. I can't see why someone would have gone to the bother of hiding it so well, or why someone would pay Dad to get it.

Dad comes over to join us, and the three of us stare at the little bundle in the dim blue light.

'How did you find it?' he asks.

'It kind of called to me,' I say.

'The customer was right,' Dad mutters. 'I did need you to find it.'

I recall the instruction that I *must* help Dad with the pickup. Me. Not Dad or Aria. They knew that I would hear it. They knew that I would be the one to find it. *What connection is there between me and this parcel?* A shiver runs down my spine.

Dad lifts the parcel from my outstretched palm and carefully tucks it into his backpack. A low moaning starts up instantly.

'Oh no, not again.' I put my hands up to cover my ears.

'What?' he asks.

'Can't you hear that noise?'

Dad and Aria shake their heads.

'That's weird. It's like someone crying. It started as soon as Dad picked up the parcel.'

'Curious,' Dad says. He looks at me, his head tilted and his brow furrowed. I get the distinct feeling that he knows something. Dad retrieves the bundle from his backpack and passes it back to me.

'Take it, but don't …' he says.

'… don't open it,' I chant. 'We know Dad. Don't open the parcel. Never, ever open the parcel. We get it.'

The instant I take the parcel from him, the moaning stops. I hold it up to my ear. It gives off a faint whooshing sound, like you get from a seashell. I feel myself drifting into a trance. I drag myself back to reality.

'That's weird,' I say. 'Listen to this.' I hold the parcel out to Aria.

She lifts it to her ear, screwing up her face in concentration, then shrugs. 'Nothing.'

'I can hear the sea in it,' I say. 'I knew this parcel was special. It's something to do with the Sea-Tamers.' Under my breath, I add, 'And Morgan.'

'I think you should carry it back to the boat for us.' Dad laughs, but his eyes are cold.

I shove the parcel into my pocket and push the unanswered questions out of my head.

We step out of the cave. A gang of bikers surrounds us, the engines of their mud-splattered off-road bikes growling, their headlights blazing in the twilight.

'Bounty hunters. Run!' I shout, sprinting off into the trees. *How did they find us?*

'How did they get here?' Aria pants. 'Is there another route we don't know about?'

'There must be,' I say. 'They couldn't have brought those bikes up the path we came along. Maybe there's a tunnel through the mountain?'

'Earth-Wanderers,' Dad mutters. 'Always digging.'

Dad trips on a tree root and falls. I turn back.

A motorbike spins, churning up clouds of dust and cutting us off.

'Go!' Dad yells. 'Leave me.'

'I'm taking him hostage,' the leader calls, getting off his bike and striding towards Dad. 'Get the kids,' he shouts to the other bikers.

Out of the oasis, we charge down the steep mountain path.

The bikes crash through the undergrowth and onto the narrow path right behind us. There's no escape. We can't out-run them.

A huge gust of wind springs up from nowhere and blasts the mountainside.

Caught in the unexpected gust of wind, one of the bikes loses control, skids on the slippery gravel and crashes into the others, sending them all flying like dominoes over the cliff edge. We watch in shocked horror as the bikes bounce down the mountainside, shattering into pieces.

'We need to help Dad,' I say, grabbing Aria's hand and sprinting back towards the pool.

Muscles bulging, Dad faces the thug, the bike

held high above his head. 'How did you find us?' he demands.

'People here are easily "persuaded" to talk,' the biker sneers.

'Well, take this as a warning.' Dad flings the bike to the side. The gang leader shoots a look at Dad, his mouth twisting, but he backs away. 'This isn't over, Ragnar,' he spits, picking up his bike. He leaps on, kick starts it and zooms away.

Dad dusts himself off. 'I knew this island was trouble,' he grumbles as the biker disappears in a cloud of dirt and fumes.

He looks at us. 'How did you lose the others?'

'The wind came up, and it blew them over the cliff,' Aria mumbles.

'Lucky,' Dad says. I'm sure I see him wink at Aria.

Night brings only a thin sliver of moon so it's too dark to start the descent now. We set up camp by the pool. Aria grabs her bow and arrow and heads into the woods, tossing me the fire starter kit on the way past.

I scout around the area, gathering enough dried branches and twigs to build a campfire. I clear a patch on the ground and make a ring of stones. In the middle, I place a few shreds of the silver birch bark. Leaning back so I don't get burnt, I strike the flint stick as hard and as fast as I can. Sparks rain down onto the bark. Wispy black smoke coils into the air as the bark catches alight, giving off a faint aroma of natural tar. Gradually, I add twigs and other bits of kindling, all the time fanning the embryonic flames until it builds up into a decent fire. Once it's burning brightly, I sit back and rub my hands in front of the crackling flames.

From the trees around the oasis, strange noises fill the night sky. Thankfully, our fire will keep any creatures away.

Aria reappears with two rabbits for supper. It feels like a feast.

As we settle down for the night, I pull Dad aside.

'That gust of wind when we escaped from the bikers was weird,' I say. 'Unnatural. Did Aria make it? Does she have powers too? Is she one of the other blood-magic children that you mentioned?'

'Yes, you're right,' he nods. 'She does. Or she will when she is twelve.'

'Why didn't you tell me before?'

'When Aria was born, the clan elders were worried that we would have responsibility for two of the blood-magic children. Some of them thought it was too risky. Others thought that the way we lived, always moving and hiding, was still safe. They argued amongst each other for a long time. Eventually they agreed that Aria could stay with us.

We had to promise not to tell either of you the truth about the other until you had both gained your full powers.'

'I remember when you told me there was one blood-magic child from each clan, you were going to say something else. You very nearly told me then, didn't you?'

'Almost, but I was scared the elders might take you away if they found out I had broken my promise.'

'It's different if I guess though, isn't it? They can't take me away if I work it out myself.'

Dad nods.

'If there's only one child from each clan, she can't be a Sea-Tamer. I guess she's an Air-Rider since she made that wind.'

'That's right.'

'Does she know?'

'Yes, but I made her swear to keep it secret, even from you. I'm sorry. She had to.'

'How did she make the wind though?' I ask, confused. 'She's still only ten?'

'Being around you seems to have triggered her magic early, so I started some basic training with her.'

'Please could you teach me too?'

'No, Finn. I'm sorry. I can't. I'm not a Sea-Tamer. But you're right. It is time you started training. We need to find you a teacher. We should have done it already, but I wanted Isolda to help you choose the right person. We'll work it out though, I promise. Now go to sleep.'

My dreams that night are full of magic.

SEVEN

STORM

The fire has dwindled to embers, but I get it going again and prepare three mugs of strong, sweet, black tea while we tidy up the camp.

Before we leave, I pour some water over the fire and stamp it out.

It's much easier going down than it was climbing up and the journey is quicker. Even so, it takes us all day, and it's late when we get back to the boat. I'm exhausted and ready to fall straight into bed.

'The bounty hunters might be back. We'd better get going now,' Dad says. 'It's a long journey to New London from here so I'll need you both to do night watches.'

Aria groans and pulls a face.

'It's OK,' I reassure her. 'We'll do them together. It'll be fun.'

I picture the night sea; the silver moon and stars reflected in the pitch-black water. I know Dad is always only half asleep when we are on watch, ready to rush on deck if we see another boat or if the wind changes direction, so there's nothing to worry about.

'Night sailing is definitely not my idea of fun,' Aria moans. 'It's just so black, so quiet. It gives me the creeps.'

She's right about the quiet; a delicious peace cloaks the night sea.

We eat dinner on deck under the stars. Despite the light wind, we make good progress. I glance at the sea. It's become so calm it's glassy, like a polished mirror, reflecting the night sky perfectly. It's beautiful, but I've been sailing long enough to recognise the signs. The calm before the storm.

'Dad, did you see anything about a storm?'

'No. There was nothing forecast,' Dad says.

We gaze at the low clouds on the horizon, skimming the peaks of land. Signs of variable winds. Change is coming.

Aria sniffs the air and frowns.

'I'm sure it's fine,' Dad says, but his face is taut.

Over the next few hours, it becomes clear we were right to be worried. The weather forecast was wrong. The wind picks up, whipping the waves into angry white crests. Clouds cover the moon.

Our boat may be old and heavy, but it's strongly built. The dark wood creaks and groans as we're tossed about by the waves. With each breaking wave, a flood of salty seawater crashes over the deck, soaking us to the skin and making my eyes sting.

I concentrate on cutting through the waves at an angle to minimise the motion. Aria retreats to her cabin feeling seasick. Despite living on a boat all her life, she's never quite got used to rough seas. Unlike me, the sea is not her natural environment.

Dad reefs in the main sail, reducing the speed. It makes the boat a little easier to manage, but it's not enough.

The large genoa sail at the bow still pulls us around like a rag doll.

'It's too dangerous,' Dad says, struggling to control the wild genoa. 'We might capsize. I'm going to have to swap the genoa for the storm sail.'

I don't want him to go. Changing a sail in this

weather is such a difficult and dangerous task, but there's no other option. The tough little storm sail is our only hope.

Dad sets off to the front of the boat. Beyond the mast, he fades into the darkness. The wind whips his voice away. Blindly, I hold the course and hope that was what he shouted as he went forward.

Time drags on and he still hasn't come back. Fear clamps my heart and squeezes it tight. I search the sea, filled with dread. If a wave swept him overboard I wouldn't see or hear him fall, and even if I did, it would be almost impossible to rescue him in such a rough sea.

From the darkness, a shadowy figure crawls back along the deck, dragging itself against the force of the wind.

Relief floods through me. 'Dad! You're OK! I was so worried.'

Dad hauls himself back into the cockpit. I relax for a moment. That's all it takes. In that one instant, a wave catches the rudder and jerks the wheel out of my hands. It spins wildly and the boat lurches to the side.

'Gybe,' I shout, too late, as the boom swings violently across the boat, catching Dad on the side of his head. He crumples. A trickle of sticky, red blood oozes from his head. *What can I do?* I can't let go of the wheel in the storm. Not even for a second. *Is he even breathing?*

'Ariaaaa ... help me ... now ... please ... help ...'

I yell as loudly as I can over the raging storm and crashing waves.

'What is it?' she says, crawling on hands and knees up the stairs into the cockpit. Normally at this point Aria would be moaning about how seasick she feels and how much she hates sailing, but she must be able to hear the panic in my voice and doesn't complain.

Her eyes bulge as she spots Dad lying in a heap. She examines him while I explain what happened.

'He's unconscious, but the wound isn't too bad,' she says. 'I promise it won't look so awful once the bleeding stops and I clean it up. He'll be ok, he's just going to have one huge headache.'

She pulls the medical kit out from one of the lockers and deftly bandages his head up. He's far too heavy for her to move him down below on her own, so she makes him as comfortable as possible on the floor of the cockpit.

While she's busy, I focus on sailing. It's almost impossible with the boat pitching and rolling so violently. One minute I'm heaving the wheel hard to port, then it's hard to starboard, and that's just trying to keep us steady. It would only take one of the giant waves hitting us full on the beam to cause us to roll, and maybe even sink. I know I can't let that happen. I won't let it happen.

I've never handled the boat on my own during a big storm before, but I know what I need to do, and I can read the sea well enough to anticipate the next assault. I grit my teeth and concentrate as hard as I can. Hour after hour we plough on through the turmoil. Exhaustion fills me. My arms are weak from the effort and my hands are numb but I keep a vice-like grip on the wheel.

We spend the rest of the night like this; Aria wedged into a corner looking pale and frightened, Dad conscious again but motionless, and me fighting with the wheel. Time stands still, the wind howls and waves batter us relentlessly. We're too tired and scared to talk.

Morning breaks and the sky starts to lighten, turning faintly pinkish. The sun creeps over the horizon and I can feel the wind get a little lighter too.

The storm sail did its job and kept us from capsizing. I forgive it for being a squat, ugly, chunk of canvas.

As the waves get less violent, Aria starts to recover from her seasickness, the colour slowly returns to her cheeks. She checks on Dad one more time, then disappears downstairs.

'What's for breakfast?' I call as she passes the galley.

'Nothing, I need to work out where we are,' she

says, plonking herself down at the chart table. 'We got totally blown off course during the storm.'

'Do you have any idea where we are then?'

'No. Most of the instruments, including the GPS, got damaged during the storm. Maybe we could use the radar, just this once?'

'No way. The radar would instantly flag up our position to everyone. Pirates, bounty hunters, trackers …. No chance. And especially not while we have a package on board.'

'OK. I'll get a rough position now and take an accurate reading from the stars tonight and work out exactly where we are then.'

I grab a packet of biscuits and start munching.

'Mum wouldn't approve of that for breakfast,' she grumbles. I get a knot in my stomach as I think, *Mum's not here*, but I don't say anything.

A pod of dolphins joins us, leaping and diving, oblivious to the horrible night we just survived. After playing in the bow wave for a while, most of the pod drifts off to find new playmates. Just three remain, racing alongside the boat. Three very familiar characters.

'Hey, Finn,' they greet me

cheerfully, their clicks and clacks translating fluently in my head. 'Did you see the size of the waves last night? They were epic.'

'Couldn't miss them,' I reply, 'since I'm on a boat in the middle of the sea. And they were not epic. They were awful. You could have warned me there was a storm coming. It wasn't in our forecast.'

'Sorry, Finn,' they say. 'We were on a mission.'

'OK super sleuths, what are you doing here then? If you're on a mission, shouldn't you be off doing something important?'

'This is our mission. You'll see. Someone wants to meet you. Follow us. This way,' they call, darting ahead.

'Who wants to meet us?' I ask.

'Wait and see,' they reply.

'Are you talking to yourself?' Aria says, sticking her head up through a hatch on the deck.

'No. Yes. Whatever,' I say.

Aria joins me on deck and checks the compass. 'How did you decide what course to steer?' she asks.

'Uhm. I'm kind of just following those dolphins,' I say. 'They told me to.'

'I can't believe we're navigating by dolphin,' Aria laughs.

'Well, until you work out where we are, it's going to have to do for a course.'

'Fair enough.'

'One other thing, they said there was someone who wanted to meet us.'

'That's strange. Did they say who?'

'No,' I say. 'They wouldn't tell me.'

'Shall I take a turn on the helm and you can get some sleep?'

With the gentle motion of the waves, such a relief after the violence of the storm, and the complete physical exhaustion, I'm rocked to sleep in seconds. When I wake up, the sun is high in the sky. I climb the mast and clamber into the crow's nest. The view from up here is amazing. I look down at the outline of our boat and silently thank her for keeping us safe during the storm last night.

I scan the horizon. I can just make out a small island. The dolphins appear to be heading in that direction. Despite the solid construction of our boat, the streamlined shape slices cleanly through the waves so we're faster than you might expect. Even so, the island is still several hours away.

I take a turn on the helm whilst Aria dozes. As we get closer, I can see the shore. Palm trees sway in the breeze. Birdsong fills the air. A broad sandy bay curves around a turquoise lagoon, protected by sharp coral reefs. It appears to be uninhabited.

The dolphins guide us through the coral maze without a scratch and we drop the anchor. The holding is good and the anchor ploughs securely into the seabed. I allow myself a little flush of pride

– I made it through the storm and to a safe harbour. A cloud quickly returns though; Dad is injured, and being on an unknown desert island is never good.

Dad stands up woozily. 'Where are we? Why are we anchored?' Without waiting for an answer, he wobbles his way downstairs to his cabin.

Aria points at some coconut trees on the shore. 'Whose turn is it to get them?' she asks.

'Definitely yours. I went last time.'

Aria shrugs, 'Are you sure?' She lifts the wooden rowing boat off the deck and lowers it into the water.

'How do you do that?' I ask. 'You make it look like it's not heavy.'

'It isn't, to me,' she says. 'I feel like the air supports it.' I think of the way Dad lifted the bounty hunter's motorbike.

With just a few fluid strokes, she rows to shore, hops into the shallow water and drags the rowing boat up onto the beach.

She scampers up a tree and fills her backpack with giant, green coconuts. She shimmies back to the ground, tosses the overflowing backpack into the bottom of the rowing boat, pushes it into the water, picks up the oars and cuts her way back to the *Alcina*.

She passes over a coconut so I can make a hole in it for her, and another for myself. I tip the coconut up over my mouth and pour the cool, fresh liquid down my throat in great gulps.

'I'll take this one down to Dad,' she says picking up another and heading below decks, 'If he's awake.'

Suddenly, I realise there's someone standing in the water in front of me. *Where did they come from?* I didn't hear anyone wading out to the boat.

I must be hallucinating.

The character is not so much standing in the water as standing *on* the water.

EIGHT

WITCH-DOCTOR

'Aria, could you come here, please? We've got a visitor… I think,' I call.

My eyes are glued to the woman. Tattoos cover her body; the images crawling across her bone white skin as if they were alive. Her black hair hangs in gnarled dreadlocks, entwining an assortment of bones and beads, like a witch-doctor, or voodoo-priestess. Animal skins cling to her curves; claws and teeth still attached. Magic radiates from her, her outline almost shimmering. Terrifying, yet strangely captivating.

The witch-doctor stretches out her hand. She's close enough to touch me. Instinctively, I pull back. I want to run away and hide, but she smiles and her whole face lights up.

I take a deep breath before speaking, 'Who are you?'

Without consciously deciding to, I tentatively reach for her, her strangeness drawing me in like a magnet, but just when I should touch her, my fingers glide straight through. I snatch my hand back and clasp it to my chest.

'She's a ghost,' Aria exclaims.

The mysterious lady doesn't speak, but turns and points inland, gesturing at us to follow.

'What should we do?' I ask Aria. 'Do you want to follow her?'

'No, look at her! And we don't know who she is.'

'She hasn't attacked us … yet.'

'I guess.' Aria wrinkles her nose. 'She could have snuck up on you if she wanted to kill you, or cast a spell and we'd both be dead.'

'Exactly,' I agree. 'I want to see where she's going. I think we should follow her, just for a bit.'

'Are you sure?' Aria's voice wavers.

'We can always turn back if we don't like it,' I say, although I know in my heart I won't be able to. I'm drawn to this strange lady, as if bewitched. 'And we'll come back to the boat before it gets dark.' Probably another lie.

I scribble a quick note for Dad, so he isn't worried when he wakes up, and we're off.

∾∾∾

We follow the ghost woman along a dried-out river bed. Insects scuttle amongst the fallen leaves and twigs. Brittle, brown fronds crack under our feet.

She stops in front of a small hut. The walls are woven out of vines and it's thatched with giant banana plant leaves. It's so well camouflaged that I would have walked straight past without noticing it.

Her exact double steps out from the hut and merges into the ghost-like figure we'd been following, leaving us facing a solid, real person. I'm not sure if that makes me feel safer or not.

'Come in,' she says, her voice as dark and rich as treacle. She holds back a screen made from strings of beads and shells. 'We have a lot to discuss.'

I take a deep breath and step through the screen. The beads and shells jingle as they fall back across the entrance plunging us into semi-darkness. A jumble of rugs and multi-coloured cushions fill the hut. The only light comes from dozens of flickering candles perched on ledges around the walls.

I've never seen so many objects in one place. Glittering crystals and orbs, dusty books and scrolls, rough wood carvings, and hundreds of tiny delicate models of strange creatures: beasts with wings, birds with fins, and more.

'At last. You're here. I've been waiting for years to meet you,' she says, clasping my hand.

'You have?' I ask, confused.

'Of course. I've been watching you.'

'Watching me?'

'You are the only one who can find the relic and release me.'

'Who are you? What are you talking about?' I ask.

The witch-doctor closes her eyes and takes several deep breaths, her hands clasped as if praying. Her eyes ping open. 'Let's start again,' she says. 'My name is Lisana. I was born over four hundred years ago.'

'That's impossible,' Aria says. She turns to face me, 'Coming here was a mistake, Finn. We should go back to the boat.'

Lisana whirls round as if she had only just noticed Aria. 'Wait,' Lisana says. 'Let me finish before you decide what to do. If you want to walk away then, I will accept your decision and you may leave freely, but you *must* hear me out.'

A shiver runs down my spine, but I nod.

'When I was a young girl, I was given a task. I was to be a guardian. My family were so proud of me. It was such an honour to be chosen.'

She stops. Her voice falters as if there's something she doesn't want to say. Her fingers pick at the edges of her belt, pulling the fibres loose.

I nudge her to continue, 'A guardian of what?'

Lisana draws herself to her full height and slaps her hand over her heart. 'Of a relic,' she says proudly. 'One of the most important items in the world.'

'A relic? What makes it so important?' I ask.

'The relics were created during the Last War. In their quest to rule the world, the Earth Lords tried to kill magic. Unable to defeat the Earth Lords, the clans were forced into hiding. Each one chose a sacred relic and locked their magical powers away in it,' Lisana continues.

'But the Earth Lords rule anyway,' I ask. 'What was the point of hiding the powers in a relic?'

'It bought the clans time. One day, they hope to release the magic from the relics and to rise again.'

I turn to Aria. 'Why did Mum only tell us half the story? She only told us about the clans. She never mentioned relics.'

Aria shrugs.

'The relics are a closely guarded secret. It was safer for you not to know about them,' Lisana says to me.

Lisana turns to Aria and leans down, her face just millimetres from Aria's, her breath hard and fast. Aria's bright blue eyes glaze over, unfocussed. 'Safer for both of you, I think. What is it that I sense within you …' Lisana sniffs the air, wolf-like.

Aria shuffles uncomfortably and stares at the floor, pursing her lips.

'A Rider,' Lisana says, standing bolt upright. 'Yes … An air-rider. The first blood-magic Rider in centuries.'

Aria lifts her eyes from the floor and looks at me.

'It's OK', I say to her. 'I know the truth. I guessed you made the strange gust of wind that knocked the bikers off the cliff near the cave. I asked Dad about it.'

Aria smiles. 'I wanted to tell you ages ago, but Dad made me promise not to say anything,' she says.

'Good,' Lisana interrupts. 'Your powers are already growing. But you are not my concern. Yours will be a different quest. You two, a sea-tamer and an air-rider, are the Relic Hunters. It is your destiny. Together, you can, and you must, change history. You must find the relics and free the clans.'

'If magic is just hidden in these relics, not gone, does that mean it can come back?' I ask.

'Yes, it can. The guardians were appointed to protect the relics until the time was right to release the magic,' Lisana says. 'That's why Sir Waldred must find and destroy the relics. Only then will magic truly be lost and the Earth Lords rule forever unchallenged.'

'So, there are two ways to restore magic to the world? Through the blood-magic and through the relics.'

'Not exactly. The blood-magic lives in just a few. Those few must use their relic to restore magic to the rest of the clan. With your help,' Lisana continues, 'the Sea-Tamers can be reborn. You, Finn, must free them.'

Responsibility presses down on me. *Can I do it?*

She stoops down in front of me until our faces are level. I feel her energy pushing inside my head, pulsing, swirling bright red, deep green, and vivid purple. The room spins then dissolves. Images flood into my mind. Children playing, weaving water, climbing clouds …

I put my hands up defensively. She snaps her fingers and the images vanish but I feel a tentative thread still joins us, as delicate as spider silk.

I stumble out of the hut, collapse onto the dirt and vomit. Inside, I hear Aria shout at Lisana. After a few minutes, Aria emerges. She crouches down beside me, helps me to my feet, then half carries me back into the hut.

Lisana kneels before me and takes my hand. 'I didn't mean to scare you, but I had to show you the truth. You had to understand. We need you.'

'I know. I saw. I understand. I'll do my best,' I say.

Tears spill from her eyes. She rubs them away with the back of her hand, leaving a streak on her face.

'What's wrong?' I ask. 'I said I'd try. I can't promise anything more than that.'

'I know. These are tears of happiness. I have waited so long to hear you say those words. You've given me hope again. You see, I was a terrible choice of guardian,' she says through the tears. 'I failed. I lost the relic. The elders cast me out of the clan, they banished me. I brought such shame on my family.'

'I'm sure losing it was an accident,' I say. 'Maybe we could help you find it?'

Lisana's face hardens. 'Don't you see? It has been found.'

'Found?' I ask. Subconsciously, I pat the parcel in my pocket. *How does she know about it?*

NINE

SECRETS

'The relic … it called to you, didn't it …' Lisana says, pacing up and down like a caged tiger. 'You've found the relic. And you've brought it here. We have no time to lose. You must take it to the elders.'

'Err …' I start.

Lisana's eyes flick towards my pocket, the one where the parcel is nestled. 'Yes, my relic …' she says, then stops, her eyes fixed on my pocket. The silence stretches, tension building like an elastic band, ready to snap back at any moment. A claw-like hand reaches towards me.

'It's not yours,' I say, ducking out of reach. 'It's mine.'

'It doesn't belong to either of you,' Aria says, planting herself between us. 'It belongs to the elders.'

'You're right,' Lisana says. 'It's just hard to resist after all these years.'

'How did you know I had it?' I ask.

'It sings of the sea. It calls to me.'

Aria pulls me aside and whispers, 'That's what the voice in the cave was saying. S. E. A.' She spells the word out. 'Not S. E. E. The parcel, it really did call to you. It really is the Sea-Tamer relic.'

'She's right,' Lisana says. 'That you lived long enough to come into your powers and find it is a miracle. Kallan and Morgan made the right choice. The elders did well hiding you.'

'The elders didn't do much except cause trouble from what I can see. But Mum and Dad certainly kept me safe,' I say. 'Do you know Kallan and Morgan?'

'Yes, I knew them. We were friends once. A very long time ago, long before you were born,' Lisana says.

'Oh. I hoped you knew where they were.'

'Well, Kallan will still be with the Elders, but they haven't spoken to me since I lost the relic. I haven't seen or heard from Morgan.'

'So how did you find me then?' I ask.

'As your blood-magic started to grow, I felt you, I saw you. I sent the dolphins to watch over you. Yet you used your powers too freely, without caution. You made ripples that spread in great rings around the world. It was most unwise. Others saw you too. Sir Waldred saw you. He realised your secret. Like me, he realised you would have the power to locate the missing relic.'

I gasp. Sir Waldred is watching me? 'Dad should have told me to stop,' I protest, although I know in my heart that even if he had, I would have carried on secretly anyway. The thrill of exploring my new skills was too exciting for me to have stopped.

'You,' she continues, jabbing me with a bony finger, 'should have started training long ago. What was your father thinking, keeping you ignorant and untrained? We risk losing everything.'

'I know,' I say. 'Dad has promised to find me a teacher.'

'The elders will find the right teacher. But first we need to find the elders.'

'How do we do that?' Aria asks.

'We have no time to lose. When Finn first touched the relic back in the cave, I saw him. I saw where he was. But I'm not the only person who was watching. They're coming for you.'

'Who are coming for us?' Aria asks.

'Waldred's trackers. Now that Sir Waldred knows you have found the relic, it's a race to stop you from releasing the magic inside it.'

Trackers. My heart skips a beat. We're doomed. That elite force will pursue you to the very ends of the earth. Escape from the trackers is impossible. They always catch their targets. Whispered stories of torture and murder are passed between smugglers, but nobody knows what really happens when they catch you. Nobody lives to tell the tale. Dreading the answer, but needing to know, I ask, 'How long do we have before they get here?'

'A couple of days at most. The nearest mega-city is New Istanbul. It's only a few days' sail away so they will be close.'

The colour has drained from Aria's face turning her as white as a sheet. 'You mean we're being … h … hunted?' she stammers.

'Yes,' Lisana says with a scowl, 'hunted. The relic hunters are also the hunted. You must get away before they reach here. Open the parcel.'

I hesitate.

'Wait,' Lisana urges, rummaging in a trunk. 'Use these.' She passes me a massive pair of shark-skin gloves, far too big for a twelve-year-old boy. 'These should help muffle the signal and make it more difficult for you to be tracked.'

Fumbling through the gloves, I pull the parcel from my pocket and place it on the floor of the hut between us. I hesitate. It wouldn't be the first time I've opened a parcel after all, despite Dad's number one rule, *Never, ever open a parcel*. This is no different, I tell myself. I can re-wrap it later and he'll never know.

I let the tatty fabric slip off. We gasp. Resting in the middle of the ancient, grubby cloth is a giant, black pearl. It shimmers with a myriad of colours.

'At last, the Sea-Tamer sacred relic has returned,' Lisana whispers. 'For years, I scoured the remotest corners of the globe. Where was it? How did you find it?'

'Dad was asked to pick it up.'

'By whom?' Lisana asks.

'He claims he doesn't know, but I think he does,' I say. 'I think he has a secret.'

'You never said, how did you lose it?' Aria asks.

'It was stolen from me.'

'Why would someone do that?'

'To protect it from Sir Waldred. And from me. They knew … knew that … that I was in love with him. My love put the relic in peril. So they stole it and hid it somewhere it would never be found.'

'But how did they get it from you?'

'They tricked me. I thought we were friends.'

'You mean you know who took it?'

'Yes, I'm afraid I do.'

'Who was it?'

'Isolda and Morgan.'

'Mum?' Aria cries. 'Have you seen her?'

'Morgan, again,' I whisper.

'I haven't seen either of them. I don't know where they are.'

'It's all your fault,' Aria explodes. 'If it wasn't for you, Mum would still be here. I bet she left because of you.'

'Aria, it can't be Lisana's fault that she disappeared. Lisana lost her relic long before either of us was even born.'

Aria scowls at me. 'I'm sure it's all connected. I'm sure this is why she vanished.'

'Aria, there are lots of reasons why she might have left us. You have to let her go.'

'I won't. She's not dead. I would know,' Aria says, wringing her hands.

'Let me search for her,' Lisana says. 'Maybe I can see if she has crossed to the spirit world or if she still lives.'

She spreads her fingers on the table. Her eyes cloud over. Assorted beads and bones in her dreadlocks clatter onto the table as her head drops forward. Her breathing slows.

Aria looks at me. I shrug. The air grows heavy. Sweat trickles down my back. Aria wipes her brow. Suddenly, a cool breeze whirls through the hut. Lisana sits bolt upright.

'She is here. In this world.'

Aria bursts into tears, shaking uncontrollably, 'I knew she was alive. Where is she?'

'I cannot see where she is,' Lisana continues. 'Something is blocking my vision. Something powerful.'

'We need to find her,' Aria says, between sobs.

'You will,' Lisana says. 'But not yet. We need to deal with this first.'

Aria reaches out to the pearl. 'Don't touch it,' Lisana warns her. 'The Sea-Tamer needs to unlock the secrets within.'

Still wearing the hideous gloves, I raise the pearl and peer into it. Images form on the swirling surface, but dissolve before I can make them out.

'What do you see?' Lisana asks.

'I can't see anything. It's all blurry. Pictures kind of move over the pearl, but each time I think I can see what one is, it vanishes.'

'Concentrate. You'll see,' Lisana says. 'You just need to focus.'

'Concentrating is not his strongest skill,' Aria snorts, fully aware that I have very limited patience.

I look back down at the pearl in my hand. Images shift like quicksand. 'It's hopeless. I can't make any sense of it. I will never see anything. It's too difficult,' I moan. Despite my protests, I keep trying.

‿ↄ℔ↄ℔ↄ℔

A headache hammers at the back of my eyeballs, and I still have absolutely no idea what's in the swirls. I'm convinced they're pictures, but they move so quickly

I can never quite see them properly. Sometimes I think it's on a loop – that the scenes are repeating – but then again maybe not. Maybe I'm imagining that.

I can't concentrate any longer because my head hurts so I play with the pearl, turning it over in my gloved hands, eavesdropping on Lisana and Aria.

'We have much to do in preparation,' Lisana says. From one of the cabinets, she lifts out an ornately carved stone cube. Her back is turned to me and her voice is low, but I catch a glimpse of her handing it to Aria. I strain to hear. 'You must keep this with the relic,' Lisana murmurs.

'Keep what?' I interrupt.

'You're supposed to be concentrating on the images, not eavesdropping on our conversation,' Aria scolds.

'My head hurts.'

'Oh, sorry. I guess you need a break, and we need to talk. Come and look at this.' Aria shows me the cube, turning it over and over in her hands.

'What is it?' I ask.

'Just a box. Doesn't seem to do anything. Don't get excited, it's not one of the relics,' Lisana garbles defensively. *What isn't she telling me?*

'Can I see it?' I ask.

Aria passes it to me. I fiddle with the box, twisting it as if playing with a Rubik's cube. It springs apart into a series of odd shaped compartments connected in a long chain like a centipede.

Lisana gasps, 'I didn't know it unfolded like that.'

'Look, each compartment has a tiny keyhole,' I say. I try wiggling the compartments, but each segment is firmly locked. I screw up my eyes and squint through one of the keyholes. 'It's too small, I can't see anything.'

'I wonder,' Lisana says, rummaging in the collection of beads, strings and trinkets around her neck. She selects one and pulls it over her head. Dangling from the delicate silver chain is a small key. It swings hypnotically in front of me.

The key doesn't fit the first lock, or the second. It doesn't work. Nothing. Excitement turns to frustration. Then, just as I'm about to give up, a lid pops open.

TEN

VISION

We crowd round. Pure white silk lines the compartment, like a jewellery box.

'It's empty,' Aria says, slumping with the disappointment.

The pearl lies next to the open cube. I pick it up and push it into a dip in the silk cushion.

A crystal-clear vision blinds me. An island. Cold, windswept, and rocky. Barren except for a few, hunched over trees, clinging to a thin stony soil. A ruined castle, perched on the edge of the cliffs, lashed by a steel grey sea.

In shock, I drop the cube. It lands with a thud. The pearl spills from it and rolls across the floor. As suddenly as it appeared, the image is gone.

Lisana springs after the pearl, scrabbling around on the floor to retrieve it and laying it carefully back on the cloth.

Stunned, I rub my eyes so hard they start to water.

'What happened?' Aria asks.

'Well, I saw something. Just for a second, but this time it was crystal clear.'

'What did you see?'

'A ruined castle on an island. It looked cold so it must be in the far north.'

'And? There must be more,' Lisana says, frustration bubbling up in her voice. 'Who was there? What else did you see?'

'Nothing. That was it. Just a ruined castle. There weren't any people there. It looked like it had been abandoned centuries ago.'

Lisana paces around the hut. 'Was there anything happening there? Anything unusual about it?'

I close my eyes and scrunch up my face as I try to recreate the image in my mind. I simply can't remember any other details. 'I'm so sorry, Lisana, that's all there was.'

Aria twirls her hair, deep in thought.

I pick up the pearl again, but there's no clear image.

'The cube. Give me the cube,' I say. 'It's some kind of force field reader. I need to put the pearl in it and try again.'

'That would explain why the elders gave it to me and told me to keep them together,' Lisana says. 'I can't believe they didn't think to mention that though.' She continues muttering to herself, looking grumpy. 'It would have been useful to know what the cube actually did.'

The room freezes as I take the cube. *Will it work?*

I place the pearl back into the hollow, holding my breath.

'Yes,' I cry. 'The image is back.' I scan it for details, for any clue I missed last time. 'Got it. There's a flag on the castle, I can see it now.'

'What does it look like?' Lisana asks.

'It's flying from one of the castle turrets. It's dark blue with a white cross on it and a black circle like the pearl. There are the fins of a dolphin on the sides of the circle.'

I look at Lisana, 'Do you know whose flag that is?'

'Sorry,' she shakes her head. 'I don't know that flag.'

Dejected, I remove the pearl from the cube and place it back in the middle of its battered wrappings.

Aria and Lisana move away and talk in low voices on the far side of the hut. From what I can hear, it doesn't sound like Lisana knows anything more than what she has already told us. Her original briefing was to guard the relic – which she then lost, with vague instructions along the lines of, *when the time is right you will know what to do* – which clearly, she doesn't.

Lisana's voice rises, 'We must take the relic to the elders. You cannot take it to New London.'

'This is Dad's delivery,' Aria replies. 'We don't know who his customer is. Maybe he is taking it to the clan elders?'

'Never in New London,' Lisana snaps.

A worrying thought pops into my head. *Could Dad be working for Sir Waldred?*

I call over to them, 'I still think Dad knows more about this parcel than he's told us. It would explain why he's been all mysterious about the delivery.'

'We need to ask him,' Aria says, standing up. 'I'm going to get him. It's late and he'll be wondering where we are. Plus, I want to tell him Mum's alive.'

'Please don't tell him about the pearl until you get back here,' I say.

'OK, I won't,' Aria agrees, 'but I'm going to tell him about Mum.' She dashes out of the hut and speeds down the hill towards the boat.

Where's Aria? Why's she taking so long? I should have gone with her.

Shadows creep and crawl over the walls in the candle light. Like a blind man, I stumble outside.

Dusk settles, forcing last of the sun's rays below the horizon.

Relief floods through me as an Aria shaped figure emerges from the murky twilight. Dad marches beside her. He doesn't look happy.

'Finn, what's happened? Aria says you have something to tell me.' He looks around. 'How did you find this place? What are you doing? Whose hut is that?'

Not sure where to start with such a barrage of questions, especially since they are entirely the wrong questions, I pull aside the beaded curtain and step into the hut. Dad and Aria follow. I point guiltily to the cloth, lying discarded on the floor. Dad looks down and sees what I am looking at …

'The parcel,' he says. 'Who opened it? You know you must never …'

'Yes, we know the rule, Dad, but …'

'No,' he says, glaring at me. 'No buts. You must never, ever, open a parcel. How many times do I have to say it?'

'I had to, Dad. You knew there was something special about this parcel, and that it had something to do with me. Didn't you?'

'You still had no right to open it.'

'Well I did. You were right. I am connected to it. It's the Sea-Tamer relic …'

'What? Who told you about the relics?' Dad says, his voice shaking.

Until this point Lisana has been standing quietly in the darkest corner of the hut, her head down so her face is lost in shadow. Now, she draws a deep breath, pushes her hair back and softly steps forward into the candle light. Dad notices her for the first time. His jaw drops, speechless.

'I did,' Lisana says. 'There's more at stake than you can ever imagine.'

ELEVEN

BETRAYED

Dad recovers from the shock. 'Lisana? How is this possible? How did you find us? The elders will not be happy. They didn't want you to find Finn. Why can't you just leave us alone?'

'I had to find the relic, but you seem to have found it for me.' She points a thin, bony finger to the bundle of cloth on the floor. 'Do you recognise that?'

'No,' Dad shakes his head. 'It can't be … It can't be your relic. That's impossible.'

Lisana shrugs, 'It never ceases to amaze me how often the impossible turns out to be perfectly possible. And, yes, here it is. The question is, how did you find it?'

Dad's eyes sink to the floor. 'Customer order,' he mumbles.

'Bit of a coincidence, isn't it? Of all the smugglers in the world, you get the order to deliver my relic?'

'He is the best smuggler though,' Aria says proudly.

'Best or worst. It's certainly not by chance that he has it. Ragnar, who is the customer?'

'I … I can't say,' he stammers.

Lisana places her hands on his cheeks and Dad's eyes glaze over. Lisana scowls. The flickering flames from the candles shoot straight up into the air, the earth shakes. After a few moments, she pulls her hands back and claps them together. He slumps onto the dirt floor. Aria runs to help him.

'Traitor,' Lisana spits. 'How could you?'

Dad pulls himself shakily up onto his knees, leaning heavily on Aria. 'I'm sorry. I had no choice.'

'There is always a choice,' Lisana snaps.

'Not this time. They have Isolda,' Dad says.

'Who has Mum?' Aria asks, the colour draining from her face.

'Sir Waldred,' Dad says, his eyes dropping to the floor. 'That's why I agreed to the job. I had to.'

Tears scratch at the back of my eyes. I blink them away.

'They're holding her hostage?' Lisana asks.

'Yes. They knew the relic was hidden in the cave but they couldn't find it. They needed a Sea-Tamer, they needed Finn, to locate it. I would never have agreed, but they were going to kill Isolda. I must take it to Sir Waldred to save her. I'm sorry Lisana. There is no other option.'

'No,' Lisana says, planting her hands on her hips. 'We can't do that. We must take it to the elders.'

'We have to save Mum,' Aria says. 'Dad's right.'

'But it doesn't belong to Sir Waldred.' Lisana's voice rises. 'And think of the consequences. The Sea-Tamer clan will be lost forever. The whole world will suffer. Could you live with being responsible for that?'

Dad paces up and down. He halts, stamping his foot like a big full stop. 'I can't sacrifice Isolda. She's done nothing wrong. We must deliver it as planned.'

We can't win. If we fail to make the delivery, Sir Waldred will kill Isolda. If we make the delivery, the Sea-Tamer's are lost forever. And somewhere in the middle of this nightmare is Morgan. *I can't win.*

Outside, cicadas chirp and birds sing, but inside a restless silence fills the hut.

'Maybe we *can* do both,' I say. 'I have a plan, but it would be very dangerous. You won't like it.'

'Go on, tell us,' Dad says.

'We deliver a fake pearl to New London and take the real pearl to the elders.'

'That's too risky,' Dad says. 'They'll spot it's a fake and kill us all.'

'But Sir Waldred has never seen the pearl before,' I point out. 'He doesn't know what it should look like. We just need to make it look convincing. Right?'

'True, he has never seen the relic,' Lisana says. 'But it's very dangerous. If he spots it's a fake, Ragnar is right. He'll kill us all.'

We lapse back into silence, buried in our thoughts.

'We have to try it,' I say eventually. 'It's the only plan we have. Maybe it will work. Just maybe.'

With a flurry of activity, Aria and I search Lisana's hut for a suitable fake pearl. Despite the myriad of objects crammed into the hut, there's nothing remotely pearl-like.

I flop down onto a cushion. 'It's useless. How do you make a fake pearl?'

Aria scratches her head. 'We're looking in the wrong place,' she says, her face brightening. 'Do you remember a couple of years ago we were supposed to deliver those strange marbles, the antique Chinese baoding balls?'

'Yeah, the owner never collected them. They'd be perfect to make a fake pearl.'

'That's what I thought. They should still be in one of the storage lockers.' With that she's up and out of the hut, sprinting back to the boat.

It's pitch dark by the time she reappears, panting and sweaty, her breath ragged. 'Look, I've got them. It took ages to find them, the boat is such a mess.'

'Compared to your room, the whole world is a mess,' I tease.

She gives me a withering look, and holds out a heavily embroidered, emerald green, satin box. Inside are two smooth black onyx balls.

'They don't look anything like the pearl,' I say, my heart sinking. 'It's not going to work.'

Aria is not deterred. 'I already thought of that. This is the clever bit.'

She tips her backpack upside down and a selection of nail polish bottles tumble onto the table. She picks a few colours and paints a swirly design on the first ball.

'It's OK, but not brilliant,' I say.

She picks up the second ball. 'Lisana, I need a tray, please.'

Lisana produces a silver tray. She grimaces as Aria pours nail polish over it, ruining it. Aria rolls the ball around in the pool of polish, allowing the swirls to evolve naturally.

'What do you think? Will it work?' Aria asks, waving the finished "pearl" in the air to dry.

'It has to,' I say.

'Maybe,' Dad says, shaking his head.

'What's the plan for the route?' I ask Dad. 'Should we go to New London or deliver the real one first?'

'New London,' Dad says. 'We can't be late with the delivery or they might suspect something is up.'

Everyone nods.

'Delivery is to the Strand Station, part of the old underground tube network,' Dad continues.

'Lisana, where do we take the real one?' Aria asks.

'To the elders,' Lisana says.

'Yes, we know that, but where exactly? Do you know where headquarters is currently?' Dad asks. 'I guess they still move every few years for security reasons.'

'I don't know where HQ is now. They haven't summoned me since I lost the relic,' Lisana mumbles to the floor. 'The elders never gave me instructions. They just said when the time was right, the pearl would show me the way.'

'What is it with these elders that they can never give simple instructions?' Aria says, clenching her fists.

'It doesn't matter,' I say. 'The pearl did show us the way. My vision. It wants to go to the castle.'

'Well, that's not very helpful, is it?' Lisana says. 'We don't know which castle. It will take years to search all the ruined castles in the northern seas.'

'We can work out where the castle is though,' Aria says. 'If we all work together.'

'Don't forget about the flag,' I say. 'That'll help us too.'

'There must be a clue somewhere in here,' Aria says, pointing around the hut.

Lisana goes to a cabinet and pulls out a bundle of manuscripts. Blowing a thick layer of dust off, she shoves them in front of us. 'Start looking. We don't have any time to waste.'

At first, we make good progress, flying through the papers, confident the flag and castle will be there. Hours pass, and we still have no clues.

The floor of the hut is strewn with discarded papers, but the stack of ones that we have yet to look at is still way bigger.

Enthusiasm turns to frustration.

It's almost morning by the time an exhausted Aria stabs her finger triumphantly at a picture on one of the pages. 'I think I've found it. This is what you saw, right?'

'Yes. That's the castle, and it's got the flag too.'

Lisana peers at the manuscript. 'Hmm. It doesn't say where it is though. And I don't recognise it,' she says, passing it on to Dad.

'Oh,' Dad says. 'Yes, I do know where that is. I grew up near there. It's Castle Gylen, in Scotland. But the island is deserted, nobody has lived there for centuries.'

'Perfect for the elders then. That must be it,' Lisana says.

As we finalise the plan, I hope the vision is not a wild goose chase.

'Can we go now?' I ask, impatiently.

'At first light,' Dad says.

Waiting for the sun to come up we try, unsuccessfully, to sleep.

'You must go now. There's no time to lose,' Lisana says as dawn breaks, ushering us towards the door.

We're halfway out of the hut but something stops me. I turn back to Lisana. 'Will you come with us? It's time you left this island and started to be a guardian again.'

'Thanks,' she says, beaming. 'I'd love to. And maybe I can repay you for all the trouble I have caused.'

Lisana takes a last look around her hut and grabs a few items. She hands one to each of us.

First, she holds out a large sea-green cloak for me. 'Walrus skin,' she says. 'This will allow you to swim even deeper and longer under water, and without getting cold.'

I lift the cloak over my shoulders. It hangs around me in big folds, piling around my feet. I can't imagine swimming in something so heavy. 'Are you trying to drown me?'

She tilts her head to the side, looks at me quizzically, and turns to Aria. In her hands rests a pure white, feathered dream-catcher. 'Any dark magic will get trapped in here,' she says.

Aria gasps. 'It's beautiful. I'm going to hang it above my bed.'

Finally, she hands Dad a loaf of bread. 'It's everlasting,' she says. He takes a bite. Nothing happens, the loaf doesn't grow back. 'Gotcha! It's just regular bread!' she says. Aria and I both start to giggle. The laughter breaks the tension, but it doesn't last. Her face quickly clouds over again.

She doesn't say anything aloud, but I catch her staring into Dad's eyes, and see him nodding softly. Neither of them utter a word but I know something passed between them. *Is she a telepath?*

We leave the hut in silence, Aria and I clasping our unusual gifts, and Dad looking grim.

TWELVE

HUNTED

Lisana grins as she clambers onto the *Alcina*. 'Nice boat.'

'Thanks. It's a bit big for us to sail on our own. We manage, but ...' Aria says, hesitating before adding, 'it was easier when Mum was here.' Her shoulders slump.

'We'll find her, don't worry. And you've got me to help on the boat now too.'

We're quickly out of the bay and on our way. The sun is high in the sky and the wind is perfect. Luckily Dad has managed to fix the navigation instruments. The course to New London to deliver the fake pearl is set.

'Can we come with you into New London to do the delivery?' I ask.

'No, I think it's better if I go alone, as if it was

a regular delivery,' Dad says. 'But I won't give over the fake pearl until I know Isolda is safe.'

We pore over maps of New London, tracing out the streets which twist and turn around the station like a pile of wriggling worms. *Be prepared*, as the boy scout motto says. We locate an original blueprint of the old Strand Underground Station. Dad plans his escape route, just in case they spot the pearl is fake before he gets Mum back.

Lisana prowls on deck, even more restless than usual. She screws up her eyes and sniffs the air. 'Trackers. They're close.'

My stomach lurches at the thought.

'I thought we were safe from them. Why would the trackers be after us? Surely, if it's for Sir Waldred he wouldn't send the trackers? I mean, there's no point in them chasing us since we're bringing it to him anyway, is there?' I ask.

'No. They are coming for you. I can feel them,' Lisana says, her face dark and brooding.

'But why would they do that? It makes no sense,' Aria says, raising her eyebrows.

'When did Sir Waldred ever honour a bargain?' Dad says. 'If the trackers can steal the relic from us before we get to New London, then he doesn't need to release Isolda. He'll force us to do something else to free her. Another ransom to be paid in exchange for her life.' He looks around the room, his gaze lingers on Aria, his eyes full of worry. 'We can still be of great use to him.'

Tension hangs in the air. We take turns on watch from the crow's nest at the top of the mast. None of us say it aloud, but we all know it's only a matter of time before they catch up with us.

Darkness has not yet surrendered to daylight and Aria is on look-out. I'm asleep on deck, too restless to be confined to my cabin.

'What's that?' Aria calls down to me, pointing to a speck on the horizon.

'Probably just another fishing boat,' I say.

'I can't see any rigging and it's too far offshore for a fishing boat, isn't it?'

I scramble up the mast and hop into the crows-nest beside her. 'You're right, it's the wrong shape for a fishing boat. Trackers?'

We watch the speck together for a while.

'It's getting closer,' Aria says. 'And it's coming straight for us. Fast. We'd better get Dad.' We slide down the mast as if it was a fireman's pole.

Nervously, the three of us line up in a row along

the stern of the *Alcina*. As it gets closer, we recognise the unmistakable hulking shape of a jet-ship swiftly closing the gap between us.

We spring into action.

'They're gaining on us. We need more speed,' Dad cries.

The wind carries the smell of burning fuel from their engines. It catches the back of my throat and makes me cough. Since the Last War, fuel has been rationed. Only trackers and bounty hunters use it so wastefully.

They're close enough now for me to see the cannons on their deck.

'Faster,' Aria yells. 'They're going to fire at us.'

Lisana appears, rubbing the sleep from her eyes. 'No, they won't fire, they don't want to sink us. They want to catch us. They want the pearl.'

I take the helm and Dad adjusts the sails to give us more speed. The extra wind in the sails forces the boat to lean steeply over to one side. Things slide off the surfaces below decks and crash to the floor. But I also feel the speed pick up: seven knots, eight knots, nine knots. We're flying along, but I glance back. It's not enough. They're still getting closer. There's no way we can outrun a jet-ship.

If only we could surf, I think, panicking. *That would make us totally uncatchable.*

The sea churns behind us.

'What's that?' Aria points at a giant wave, building

from nothing, right behind us. 'Oh no, please not now. We can't get hit by a tidal wave,' Aria cries, fear making her voice quiver.

The wave grows. I feel it catching up with us, lifting us high up into the air, carrying us along. The salty sea-spray stings our eyes. We're perched on the crest of the monstrous wave. When it breaks, we'll be smashed to pieces. There's nowhere to go but down into the depths of the ocean.

Dad grabs the wheel from me but there's nothing he can do; we can't turn around, and in front of us the sea opens like a vast chasm. He holds the boat steady. His face a grim mask.

But the wave doesn't break, it keeps driving forward, pushing us along with it.

Lisana scans the sea. 'Interesting,' she mutters, looking sideways at me. 'It's you,' she whispers. 'You're doing this.'

'Huh? I promise I didn't do anything.' *But I thought about it.*

'Even more interesting. Subconscious action, a mere thought ...' Lisana says.

How did she know that? Did she read my mind?

'An ancient talent ...' she continues. 'If you can do that without training ... I wonder what you might be able to do in the future ...' Lisana's voice trails off.

Aria is dancing about at the back of the boat, watching the jet-ship. 'We're losing them,' she cheers. 'They've no chance of keeping up with us while we're surfing like this.'

Surveying our rather precarious position, Lisana nudges me and hisses under her breath, 'Finn, don't stop doing whatever it is you're doing, or not doing.'

Surf faster.

I daren't look.

'They're falling behind … yes … yes, they are. They're getting smaller. They can't keep up. We're outrunning a jet-ship,' Aria sings.

Only once the jet-ship and its crew of trackers are left far behind do I relax. As I do, the wave slowly subsides until it's nothing more than a gentle splash on the hull.

'That was totally amazing,' Aria says.

'Indeed. It was a happy piece of luck there was a freak wave, just here, at this particular moment,' Lisana says, oozing sarcasm and looking sideways at me.

'Finn, did you make that wave?' Aria asks, clocking the sarcasm in Lisana's voice.

'Maybe,' I mutter, blushing.

'Wow,' Aria says. 'I didn't know you could do that.'

'It saved our lives,' Lisana says. 'And the other good news is, provided you don't touch the pearl, they will find it much harder to track us down again. We're safe … for now.'

'There is a problem though,' Dad says. 'The fact he really did send the trackers after us means we were right. Sir Waldred has absolutely no intention of giving Isolda back without a fight. We're going to have to rescue her.'

"Welcome to New London" says the sign as we turn the boat into the Thames Estuary. Underneath, a smaller notice in scratchy writing hangs lopsidedly, *"Pirates and Smugglers Beware"*.

Rotting bodies swing from a row of gallows. My heart skips a beat. I want to look away but I can't. My eyes are locked on the corpses. The tattered remains of a skull and crossbones flutters like a cape from around the neck of one of them.

The further up the river we go, the tenser Dad gets.

We tie up in a small, murky marina just outside the city walls. A man with a long overcoat and his hat pulled down low over his eyes approaches us, 'Protection?' he growls.

Dad passes him a roll of bank notes and nods without uttering a word. The man tilts his hat and winks, a wicked glint in his eyes. He prowls back towards the warehouse. His shadow leans against the wall, lurking like a hyena, only the tip of his cigar giving a clue as to his presence.

'Stay here, all of you,' Dad says. 'I'll deliver the

fake pearl the way they instructed and find Isolda. When I get back, we'll be on the way to Castle Gylen as quickly as we can. Guard the boat, but stay out of sight … And don't talk to the man in the overcoat.'

THIRTEEN

CAPTURED

'He should be back by now,' I say. 'I think something has gone wrong. Lisana, can you sense anything?'

Lisana shakes her head. 'I fear you are right.'

Aria chews her hair nervously. 'What should we do?'

'It's up to us now. We'll have to rescue both Mum and Dad.'

'How?'

'We know the delivery was to the old Strand Station. We'll start looking there. There will be a trail.'

'But we won't even be able to get into the City? Dad had an entry permit, we don't.'

'I have a plan,' I say.

Overcoat man wipes his nose with the back of his hand as I approach.

'I need your help,' I say.

'What can I do for you?' he grunts.

I explain what I need and he sidles away.

A sharp whistle from the shadows lets me know he's returned. He holds out a package wrapped in brown paper and tied up with string.

'Thanks,' I say.

'Happy to oblige,' he says, melting back into the shadows.

Disguised as convict labourers in plain blue cotton uniforms, we join their queue to enter the city. Freshly forged identity documents, courtesy of overcoat man, stuffed in our pockets. My hands sweat as I hand the papers to the guard. He barely glances at me, stamps the first page and passes it back to me. It worked!

I shuffle forwards towards the City gates. I daren't look back to see what has happened to Aria, but hopefully the guard will show as little interest in her.

'I'm right behind you,' a voice whispers. 'Don't look round though. Keep moving with the crowd.'

We trudge along with the rest of the line onto the ferry. Not one of the workers smiles, they stare blankly ahead like robots. Years of hard labour has beaten them down. The ferry spits the group of workers out near the old parliament building at Westminster, abandoned when the Earth Lords moved into Buckingham Palace.

It's just a short walk along Embankment to the Strand from where we disembark.

As soon as we can, we slip away. With a nod and a wink, one of the convicts edges forward to fill the gap in the line left by us, covering up our disappearance. We shed the disguises, dumping the clothes in a bin.

The old Strand Station is squashed between two much grander buildings. The whole building is only a fraction wider than the door. Old-fashioned red-glazed tiles cover the front. The dark green door is blocked by a metal grill, paint peeling from years of abandonment. An arched window sits above the door, opaque with grime and pigeon droppings.

At the bottom of the metal grill, a few of the bars have been bent back, presumably the result of an attempted break-in many years ago.

The gap is far too small for an adult to squeeze through so nobody thought it worthwhile repairing the damage, but I reckon we'll fit.

'I'll go first to check it's safe,' I say. I glance around, it doesn't appear that anyone is watching us, and wriggle through the hole.

'It's safe, Aria,' I say. 'There's nobody here. Come on.'

My eyes take a few minutes to adjust to the dim light filtering through the dirty windows. A ticket office and four ticket barriers wait patiently for the long-departed customers. Beyond them I see the way down to the railway platforms. A sign warns, *"There are 193 steps in this station. Please use the escalators"*.

The escalators haven't worked in years, so we set off down the stairs. Dust works its way under my skin and makes my nose itch. The darkness gets thicker as we go deeper underground. I'm glad I remembered a torch, but the small circle of yellow light just exaggerates the shadows. I shiver.

We emerge onto the platform. The cream and green tiles form a pattern on the walls, spoiled by a dirty grey tint. Other than the sound of our footsteps, the silence is eerie. At the far end, there's a door marked *"Staff only"*.

A faint noise echoes through the station, footsteps.

'Someone's coming,' I whisper to Aria.

The footsteps get louder, running now.

'We need to hide,' Aria whispers back. 'Quick, through here,' she says, pushing me through the door.

I blink several times whilst my eyes adjust to the sudden bright light. From the dark, dirty disused platform, we've popped out into a gleaming white corridor with several doors. These weren't marked on any plans.

Which way do we go?

My heart races.

A red dot on the security camera above our heads blinks. We've been spotted.

We run, flinging open the first door and plunging through, straight into two burly men in uniforms. One grabs my arm, bending it sharply behind my back. The other does the same to Aria. They push us roughly in front of them.

'Hey,' I say, 'Let me go.' I twist myself, trying to escape from his grip, but he holds me tight.

They march us back along the maze of corridors. One of the radios strapped to the guard's belts crackles. A disembodied voice from the radio says, 'Security team alert. We have the package. We're moving out now.'

'We'd better hurry up. What do we do with these two?' asks the man holding Aria.

'Tie 'em up. We need to tell the boss there are two strange kids snooping around.'

The men shove us into one of the labs and force us to the ground. They rummage around for a roll of tape, wrench our hands behind our backs, and tie us to a bench.

I twist my hands left and right, trying to loosen the tape but it sticks to my skin and won't slip over my wrists. 'Can you get your hands free?'

'No, it's too tight,' she says. 'You?'

'No.'

'The package they mentioned must be the pearl,' Aria says, wriggling furiously. 'Let's hope they don't realise it's a fake.'

'I'm working on a plan,' I say, straining against the ties.

FOURTEEN

GIRL

'Stay still,' says a voice from behind the bench. I squirm to try and see who spoke, but with my hands tied I can't turn around far enough. I glimpse a white lab coat. 'Stop moving or I'll cut you,' the voice continues. They have a knife. I freeze. My hands come loose.

I whirl round to see our rescuer. It's a scrappy little girl with dark eyes hidden beneath a tangled mess of long, black hair. She's wearing a white lab coat that trails on the floor.

'Who are you? Why are you trying to help us?' I ask.

'I'm Pippin,' she says, squirming on her belly beneath the bench.

With a small pearl-handled pen-knife, she saws at the tape binding Aria's hands until they ping free.

'Yeuch,' Aria says, rubbing her wrists. 'That's sticky.'

'Why are you helping us?' I ask.

'Been doing a bit of research,' the girl says. 'Don't think it's right to go messing about with people in the name of science.'

'What do you mean?' I ask, surprised.

'Sir Waldred forces my dad to do experiments on people, to make them more "normal". Dad says it's cruel. How does Sir Waldred know what "normal" is? Why does he even get to decide? It's not right.'

I gasp, thinking of the blood-magic. "Normal" doesn't come close to describing that. Is that what he's trying to do? Take away the blood-magic?

The girl chatters away, 'But Sir Waldred won't listen. He just keeps on experimenting. Are you special? Guess he was going to experiment on you. Well, that's what happens to most people who get brought in here anyway. So here I am, rescuing you. You won't regret being on my team …'

'Your team?' I say, raising my eyebrows.

'Well, you aren't fully rescued yet but, once you are, you can be on my team,' she says. 'Come on. I'll show you the way out. They'll be back soon and then we'll all be in big trouble.'

'We can't leave yet,' I say, leaping up and dragging Aria behind me. 'We need to find Dad. We know they've got him here somewhere. And we think he has Mum prisoner too.' *And I need to ask Sir Waldred what he knows about Morgan.*

Bouncing up and down like an excited puppy, Pippin says, 'A mass rescue. What a great day for my campaign. I know where the prisoners are kept, follow me.'

We head off down the corridor, our soft shoes making no noise on the floor. This time we watch out for the cameras, ducking out of sight as they pan around in front of us.

I see the guards ahead, puffing and panting. We slow our pace to match. They stop in front of an opaque glass door and scan a security pass. It slides smoothly open and they step through. It closes behind them.

'We lost them. What do we do now?' I ask.

Pippin rummages in the pockets of her lab coat and pulls out a bundle of cards.

'What are those?' Aria asks.

'Security passes. People keeps losing 'em. Can't believe how careless they are,' Pippin says.

'So how come you have them if they're lost?' Aria asks.

'Depends on what you mean by *lost*,' Pippin says, a wicked grin spreading over her face. 'Did they lose 'em, then I found 'em? Or did I find 'em, then they lost 'em?'

'You mean you stole them,' Aria says, her eyes wide.

'Just borrowed. I'll give them back one day … Here we go.' Pippin says, waving one of the cards in front of my nose. It has a picture, the name "Professor Waserchen", and a barcode on it. 'Told you I 'ad a plan. This one will work.'

She holds the card up to the security pad and the flashing red light goes green instantly. 'Security really should learn how to cancel these cards permanently,' she says, grinning.

'Permanently?' Aria asks. 'Tell me you didn't hack the computer system to reactivate them?'

'Course I did! Be a waste of a perfectly good security card otherwise,' Pippin beams.

The door slides silently open into a laboratory. Rows of shelves are filled with glass bottles, all neatly labelled. The smell of chemicals wafts through the air. Equipment hums and buzzes, the noise covering us as we slip in unnoticed. Pippin pulls us sharply to the left and we crawl behind a desk.

Two scientists sit on high stools at a lab bench; one is thin with a deep scar running across his face and steel grey hair, the other is stouter, with a slick of dark greasy hair and an anxious look on his face.

They're wearing lab coats like Pippin's, but of course theirs don't trail on the ground.

The guards are standing beside the bench, shuffling from foot to foot.

'Get me the notebook,' the thin scientist barks.

The other scientist leaps to his feet as if he's just had an electric shock. He scurries across the room and starts flicking through piles of paperwork.

'That's my dad,' Pippin says, pointing at the harassed looking scientist. 'Sir Waldred is always being mean to him. He's a bully.' She pulls a face and spits on the ground in a very unladylike way.

'Is that Sir Waldred?' I whisper to Pippin, pointing at the thin scientist.

She nods.

Sir Waldred sits upright, pushes the microscope away, cracks his knuckles, and glares at the guards. 'What was so important that you felt it necessary to interrupt my work?' he asks the guards with a sneer.

'Kids. We found two kids,' stammers the first guard.

'Who?'

'Dunno. Didn't ask their names.'

'Idiots. What did they look like then?'

'Uh, there was a girl with long straight white hair and a boy with messy brown curls.'

'It's them,' Sir Waldred says, thumping the desk. 'Finally. So where are they then?'

'We tied them up and left them in the other lab. We thought …'

'Don't think. I don't pay you to think. Bring them to me, now.'

Sir Waldred leans over the microscope again, scowling, and the two guards jog away, bickering.

'It's your fault the boss isn't happy with us.'

'No, it's not. You were the one who said to tie 'em up.'

'But you said he had the package and that was more important.'

Their voices fade into the distance.

'What do we do now?' Aria whispers.

'Shhh,' I hiss. 'We need to wait and see what he does. Then we'll make a plan.'

The guards come back, red faced, empty handed, and still bickering.

'You tell him.'

'No, it's your fault.'

'Tell me what?' Sir Waldred snaps.

'The kids, they've gone,' says the first guard. 'Escaped … but I swear we tied 'em up proper.'

'Looks like they 'ad an accomplice,' says the second guard. 'The tape what we used to tie 'em up with was cut. They couldn't 'ave done it themselves.'

Pippin giggles from behind the bench, 'That's me. I'm an accomplice.' Aria clamps her hand over Pippin's mouth, smothering a snort of laughter.

'An accomplice? You mean there are even more intruders? Do I need to find a new Head of Security?' He glares at the first guard.

He turns back to Pippin's dad. 'Where is that notebook I asked for? Could you move slightly faster than a sloth?'

Pippin's dad extracts a notebook from the pile, pushing the rest of the papers aside.

'Look,' Aria whispers, pointing at the microscope which is now visible past the stack of papers. 'It's the pearl. He's studying the pearl.'

'That means Dad has been here,' I say.

'Yes, but where is he now?'

Suddenly Sir Waldred leaps up, knocking his stool over. He kicks out at it, cursing. He grabs the fake pearl and flings it across the room. It shatters into pieces.

'I guess that means he knows it's a fake,' I say.

'Bring the woman here this instant,' Sir Waldred spits at the scientist. Take that useless pair of guards with you.'

'Right away, Sir Waldred,' he says. Pippin's dad dashes away, the guards trot obediently after him.

Pippin springs to her feet. I try to grab her but it's too late.

'Leave the woman alone,' Pippin shouts, her hands on her hips. 'She's been kind to me.'

'Pippin, what are you doing here?' Sir Waldred snarls.

Aria shrinks further under the desk, bumping the table leg which makes a loud scraping sound.

Sir Waldred spins round. He heard it. He leans over the desk. Aria and I shuffle as far away as we can, but he drags Aria out by the ear.

'I see you brought your friends,' he hisses at Pippin.

I scramble to my feet.

Sir Waldred looks at us and bursts into laughter, clutching his belly. 'Well that's a surprise,' he says. 'All this time trying to catch you, and here you walk freely into my lair. Since you're here, you might as well just give me the real relic. It will be a lot less painful for you, and your family, in the long run.'

'Never,' I cry. 'Why should I? It's not yours.'

'It will be soon. Your parents will give it to me.'

'Ragnar and Isolda would never do that.'

'When they discover I have taken both of you prisoner, they will. And Morgan would without hesitating,' he taunts.

Anger rises in me and I clench my fists. 'Leave my family alone. And that includes Morgan,' I shout.

Sir Waldred's lips curl into a crooked smile. 'Haha. Morgan has already betrayed you. How does that feel?'

'She didn't mean to. You forced her.'

'Did I? Are you sure about that? Maybe she wanted to help me? Maybe she wanted revenge on the elders. Maybe I used that desire for my own purposes. Maybe she was a fool.' His face contorts with rage. 'Anyway, she's not here. She's gone on a new quest. To find the next relic. For me.' He throws his head back and roars with laughter.

Pippin's dad slinks back into the room, followed by the two guards, dragging something behind them … a woman with long straight white hair …

'It's Mum,' Aria whispers, her eyes wide. She runs and flings her arms round her.

'Make her stand up,' Sir Waldred barks. 'And get that kid away from her.'

The guards pull Aria off and yank Mum to her feet. Her eyes are bleary and heavily hooded. She looks in our direction, blinking hard as she struggles to focus. A flicker of recognition passes Mum's eyes. She starts to struggle.

'Now!' Aria says, sticking her leg out and tripping one of the guards. He lands heavily and screams in pain.

Pippin leaps onto the back of the other one. He tries to peel the little girl from his back but she clings on like a limpet. She covers his eyes with her hands and bites his shoulder.

'Ouch' he cries, stumbling blindly around the room, flailing his arms at the irritant attached to his back. He trips over the stool that Sir Waldred knocked over earlier, and lands with a crash. 'Pippin, you little rat,' he shouts, wiping away few drops of blood from the teeth shaped punctures on his shoulder as he lumbers to his feet. 'I'll get you for that.'

'You can't catch me,' Pippin chants, dancing away down the corridor.

In the chaos, Mum breaks free and runs to us. She draws us towards her and hugs us both tightly.

'Hello Pippin,' she calls. 'I see you already met my kids.'

'I rescued them,' Pippin says proudly.

'Well done, Pippin,' Mum says. Then, seeing the guard lumbering to his feet, she pushes us forward. 'Quick, follow Pippin. That way.'

I glance over my shoulder and shout, 'Faster! They're getting closer.'

'Mum, where have you been all these years? How did you end up here?' Aria pants.

'Questing. It was Morgan … I was following her. I had to stop her from destroying the world. But it was a trap, she wasn't here. I have … to warn

… Ragnar.' Mum struggles to catch her breath as she runs.

'Warn him of what?'

'Morgan …' But she looks at me and doesn't finish the sentence.

What was she going to say about Morgan?

Aria tugs at Mum's hand. 'He's here. Mum. Dad's here. We need to get him. I think he's been taken prisoner. We have to go back.'

'I know. I saw him. They were holding him in a cell just along from me. I can rescue him,' Isolda pants.

'I'm coming with you,' Aria says.

Ahead of us, a second corridor runs off to the right, sloping downwards.

Mum points to it. 'Finn, you and Pippin go that way. It'll take you to the river. Aria and I will get Dad. We'll catch up with you back at the boat. I promise.'

'We should stick together,' I protest. 'Dad always says we should stick together.'

'You must deliver the relic to the elders. Promise me you'll do that?' Aria begs.

'Relic?' Mum asks, raising her eyebrow. 'How do you know about the relics?'

'Later. It's a long story,' Aria says.

'How will you rescue Dad?' I ask.

'I know where they've taken him,' Mum says. 'And I know how to get out of here. I've been studying the layout every time they moved me, and

Pippin has given me some great tips for escaping too. You go with Pippin.'

Hand in hand, Aria and Mum sprint away.

Mum turns her head back towards me. 'Finn, if we're not back at the boat by daybreak, you need to leave us. You have to take the relic to the elders.'

'But what about you?'

'Don't worry. I know lots of people in New London. We'll be fine. We'll catch up with you, I promise.'

As she disappears around a corner, I hear her call once more, 'Please, Finn. You must deliver it safely, or it's all been for nothing.'

My heart thumps. 'I don't know if I can do it on my own,' I whisper to the empty corridor.

FIFTEEN

TUNNELS

'They're splitting up,' Sir Waldred screams. 'Guards, catch those two. I'll get the boy myself.'

Heavy footsteps pound on the stone floor, getting louder, closer and closer behind us. Corridors snake off to the left and right.

I sprint after Pippin, blindly trusting her to know the way out of this maze.

Boom. An explosion shakes the building. The tunnel ahead of us collapses in a pile of rubble. Pippin and I spin round and dart down another corridor.

Sir Waldred is right behind us, flinging blast after blast of energy at the walls.

Another huge blast and the corridor collapses. A dead end.

'We're trapped,' Pippin cries.

'Now I've got you,' Sir Waldred says, gloating. He takes a step forward.

'I'll never give the relic to you,' I shout.

'You'll have no choice,' he sneers.

I look left and right, searching for a way out. Half way between us, one of the explosions has left a crater in the ground. I glance down into the dark, jagged hole. Water bubbles inside it.

'What are you looking at?' Pippin cries. 'We can't get out that way.'

'We can,' I hiss under my breath. 'Jump in.'

'No way.'

'We need to get into the water,' I whisper as Sir Waldred takes another step closer to us. 'It's a river. It's our only chance of escape. He won't dare follow us. The Earth-Wanderers hate water. Plus, I have a walrus cloak. It's supposed to help underwater. Oh … can you swim?'

'Don't worry about me,' Pippin chirps, shrugging off the huge lab coat to reveal a threadbare grey dress and stick-thin legs. 'I'll be fine. Somehow I'm always fine.'

'The cloak will protect you.' I cross my fingers as I pull the cloak out of my backpack, hoping that's true.

I wrap the cloak tightly around us both. Clutching my pirrfu charm for luck, we count to three, run towards the hole and leap.

'Nooooo,' Waldred screams, realising just a moment too late that we aren't trying to get past him, that we're going to jump. He grabs at us as we plunge into the pool but his fingers clasp at the air.

It's deeper than I thought, and even colder. I wondered if the cloak would make us sink, but it feels weightless in the water. Underneath the cloak, Pippin is cocooned in a big air bubble.

I point to a black eel. That's a surprise. I expected rats in these tunnels, not fish. Flipping its snake-like body around, it calls to me, 'Follow, follow.' And darts off down the tunnel. I gesture at Pippin that we're moving. She nods her head. I give her the diving signal for 'OK' and kick off after the fish. *Is Pippin humming?*

After several minutes, I start to worry this was a mistake. The air bubble is rapidly shrinking. The eel urges me on, oblivious to the basic human need to breathe. Even Pippin has stopped humming.

A few more seconds and the air bubble will be gone. It's not enough. There's no obvious end to the tunnel. We're trapped. I start to panic, it's too late to turn back now. We're not going to make it. Even with my powers and the cloak, we will both run out of air in the next few minutes.

I kick harder. I won't let us die. Kick. I won't let Sir Waldred win. Kick. I will deliver the real pearl. Kick. I will find Morgan. Kick.

The tunnel turns upwards. At last, there's air above us. Pippin claws her way to the surface, coughs up some water and gulps down the fresh air.

'It stinks in here,' she says, pinching her nose closed.

We're no longer in the shiny white laboratory tunnels. This tunnel is dark and dank with a curved brick roof. I guess it was probably part of the old Victorian sewage system.

We continue swimming until the water is shallow enough to stand up in. I pull off the cloak. Underneath it, I'm surprised to find we're completely dry. I shake it out, watching the water droplets slide straight off the glossy walrus skin, and shove it in my backpack.

Knee-deep in water, my feet are sucked into the sludgy ground. I try not to think about it as I squelch through the rat-infested swamp.

'Do you have any idea where we are?' I ask Pippin, hoping that her local knowledge covers this area.

'Don't you know nothin'? It's the River Fleet. It runs underneath London all the way from Hampstead Heath and spits out into the Thames near Blackfriars Bridge. It used to be above the ground, obviously, but it got built over in about 1800. It's more of a ditch than a river.' She tugs at her leg in an attempt to free it from a particularly sticky patch.

'So can we get out at the end?' I ask.

'Dunno,' she says. 'It might surprise you, but what with all that swimming, I've never been this way before. Let's hope it's open.'

'Fingers crossed,' I say.

'Did you know, they found the remains of loads of bodies from the eleventh century in the River Fleet when they were excavating in the 1990s? They'd been decapitated,' Pippin says with morbid glee.

'Thanks for that information,' I say. 'Really reassuring.'

We trudge along, the silence only interrupted by squelches and belches from the oozing mud.

Faint rays of daylight start to filter along the underground canal. It's not exactly a relief as I can now see what we are wading through. Gross.

Pippin stops. 'Oh no,' she says, pointing ahead. 'Look, the exit. It's blocked.'

She's right. An iron grill blocks the tunnel, a sluice gate. We peer through the grill. The tunnel we're in ends about half way up the embankment wall. A few metres below us, the River Thames rushes past. Blackfriars Bridge stands to the left. So near, and yet so far.

I shake the grill in frustration. It wobbles. It's loose. I shake it harder. Several of the wall fixings are heavily rusted. Pippin grabs the bars and starts to shake it too. In a cloud of cement dust and rust, one of the fixings gives way. Thank goodness for poor maintenance. The harder we shake, the more noise we make. Surely someone will hear us but, even if they knew where we had gone after we dived into the water, the traffic thundering along Victoria Embankment above us drowns it out.

The final bolt shakes loose. The grating starts to fall. I let go, catching the back of Pippin's dress as the weight nearly pulls her over the edge. It crashes into the water below, and is carried a few metres by the current before sinking out of sight. We lean out of the hole and look down at the river below.

'Yippee! Swimming time!' Pippin says, leaping into the water.

'Wait,' I say, too late.

She bobs up and down in the water. 'Come on,' she calls up to me. 'It's lovely once you're in.'

The current is much stronger than I expected and I'm swept downstream swiftly.

I scan the water for Pippin. She waves cheerily at me.

'Isn't this the best adventure?' She does a few effortless strokes of front crawl and joins me. *How can an Earth Wanderer be so comfortable in the water?*

High stone embankments on both sides of the river imprison us in the water. It's impossible to climb out. This was a mistake.

The current whisks us under Blackfriars Bridge and towards the Old Millennium Bridge.

'Did you know they used to call that the "wobbly bridge" when they built it?' says my cheerful tour guide. 'It wobbled in the wind so badly they had to fix it right after they built it.'

Southwark Bridge and Cannon Street Bridge pass in a flash as we're swept beneath their arches.

'That's London Bridge, and that's Tower Bridge,' Pippin says, pointing them out. 'There's a really funny story about them, do you want to hear it?'

'You're going to tell me anyway, aren't you?' I say.

'It's a good one.'

'Go on then.'

'Apparently, way back in 1968, a rich tourist bought London Bridge, that's the plain brick one over there.' She points it out again. 'People say he thought he was buying the fancy Tower Bridge, which would have been way cooler. He didn't realise the mistake until it was too late, and he'd taken it all the way back to his own country, brick by brick. Obviously, London built that new bridge as a replacement.'

'No way,' I say, staring up at the two enormous bridges as we're dragged under them. 'That can't be true.'

Exhaustion takes over and Pippin stops talking.

'Don't try to swim,' I say. 'Just float with the current. We need to save our strength.'

***

Through the murky twilight, I catch sight of a familiar shape. I blink hard twice. The *Alcina*! Our boat cruises gently down the middle of the river towards us. As it gets closer, I see Lisana at the helm. I tread water and wave my arms frantically.

Lisana doesn't know we're in the water. Worse, in the dark we're practically invisible. She's heading straight for us. I start to panic. She can't see us. She's going to sail straight over us.

I yell at her. I don't care if someone hears us. The moon emerges from behind a cloud. It shines on the river, turning the dark water into liquid silver. We're caught in the light, like a rabbit in headlights. It's now or never. If she doesn't see us in the moonlight now, the current will sweep us right past the boat. 'Help,' we scream.

Suddenly, Lisana runs to the side of the boat and leans over. Then she runs back to the helm. Did she see us? Is she coming for us? The boat turns sideways. Wind spills out of the sails and the boat slows down. I breathe a sigh of relief. Lisana pulls alongside us.

'What are you doing in the water?' she asks.

'Long story. I'll explain later. Help us get out will you,' I say. 'It's freezing.'

She ties a rope to a cleat and throws the free end over the side. Pippin and I scramble up. After its dunk in the river, I realise her thin dress isn't grey, it's pale pink.

Pippin hangs over the side of the boat and vomits. She must have swallowed more of the rank river water than I thought. Round her neck, a necklace with a charm on it swings loose. She quickly tucks it back out of sight.

Pippin stares at Lisana, wrinkling her nose. 'Who's she?'

'A friend,' I say.

'She doesn't look very friendly.'

'I know, but you can't judge someone by how they look.'

'Lisana, why are you here?' I ask, changing the topic. 'You were supposed to stay in the marina.'

'I was watching you,' she reminds me. 'Been watching you for years, you know, but it's so much easier now we're connected.'

I recall the pain I felt when she read my mind in the hut. 'But I didn't feel you inside my head this time?'

'Didn't need to dig so deep. Your emotions were bubbling just beneath the surface. Saw you clear as crystal. Saw you were in a spot of bother. Thought I could lend a hand,' Lisana says. 'Your Dad said I had to stay on the boat. And I have. He didn't say the boat had to stay still though, did he?'

'You're right, technically,' I laugh. 'Although I doubt Dad will agree. I'm glad you rescued us, but I don't think Dad will be so pleased that you moved the boat.'

'Ah well, I can't help that. Anyway, where is he? And where's Aria?'

'We got separated,' I admit. 'But we found Isolda. Aria's with her. They said they'd find Dad and meet us back at the boat. At the marina, that is, not here.'

'Better head back to the marina now then,' she says. 'I don't want to get in trouble.' She looks at Pippin, 'Who's the kid?'

'Pippin. Her dad works for Sir Waldred.'

'Don't like Sir Waldred,' Pippin adds, screwing up her face in disgust.

'The kid has good judgement,' Lisana says, sticking her hand out to Pippin. 'Pleasure to meet you.' Pippin grasps her hand and shakes it vigorously.

Navigation lights are too risky to use, so we glide along the river in the pitch-dark. I tell Lisana everything that happened in the Strand Station: about seeing Sir Waldred, and finding Isolda, and how the walrus cloak helped us escape.

'Knew it would be useful,' she says, looking smug.

Overcoat man slithers out of the shadows and approaches Lisana, 'Saved your mooring, ma'am.' He nods at Lisana. 'Just like you asked.'

The marina guards don't question our comings and goings as we silently slip back into the same berth we were in earlier.

Lisana plucks a coin from a leather pouch tied to her belt and tosses it to him. He snatches it out of the air, sniffs it, and fades back into the shadows. Lisana flicks her hair and spins to face us. 'Stop gawping and get some rest.' She settles herself into a corner of the cockpit to watch for Dad.

Pippin hunts around, digs out an old sail cloth from one of the lockers, and builds a nest for herself, snuggling down as if it was a feather bed. She hums a cheerful tune that sounds vaguely like *What shall we do with the drunken sailor* and is sound asleep within minutes.

I wake to the sound of footsteps on the deck. Lisana paces up and down, peering into the weak daylight. 'We need to go,' she says. 'We can't wait for them any longer.'

'Ten more minutes,' I beg. 'They promised they'd make it.'

'Ten minutes. No more,' she says. 'With or without them, we must deliver the relic safely.'

The sun peeps over the horizon. Lisana casts off the lines and we slip silently from our berth. The marina guards barely glance at us.

They haven't made it. They must have been caught. Helpless, I watch. It's too late. Tears splash down my cheeks.

'They'll be fine,' Pippin says. 'Isolda knows loads of people here. They'll look out for her.'

I nod.

As we pull out of the berth and into the channel, the rising sun illuminates three running figures. I rush to the bow. Blinking the tears away, I see that two are tall and one is much smaller. It's them.

They sprint along the harbour wall. 'Wait for us!' they shout.

Rough stone grates the side of the boat as we pull alongside, but I don't care about the damage. They made it.

They jump on board and we turn into the channel just as the sun leaps into the sky.

'We thought they'd caught you,' I say.

'No chance,' Isolda says.

'But how did you get back to the boat so quickly?' Dad asks.

'It was Lisana, she rescued us.'

'Lisana, you were supposed to stay with the boat.'

'I did! Never left it for a second.' Lisana grins and winks at me, 'but I didn't want to miss out on all the fun.'

'You can explain that later,' Dad says. He looks at the crowd on deck and smiles. 'We have a proper crew now. All hands on deck. Set the sails. We need to get out to sea as quickly as we can. They'll be searching the river for us.'

SIXTEEN

RUINS

Sailing along the estuary, we keep watch for the trackers. The huge flood gates at the mouth of the River Thames loom ahead of us. A group of workers are at the controls. Shouts carry across the water, 'Hurry up, lads. Get those gates closed, now.'

Once the gates close, we'll be caught like a fox in a trap. Retreat is not an option with the trackers on our heels so we press forward.

One of the workers spots us coming up the river. He points, shouting, 'That's them! That's the boat!'

Huge metal plates start to slice the river in two as the flood gates judder into action.

The workers let out a cheer, 'Good work, lads. We got them. They won't make it through the gates in time.'

Dad adjusts the sails to catch more of the wind

and our speed increases. The gates continue to grind closer together.

Isolda chants something and I feel the wind gathering around us, pushing us forward. It might just be enough.

'That's it. I can't make any more,' Isolda cries as the wind drops again. 'I haven't done this in years. I'm out of practice.'

'We're not going to make it. Tack. Turn around,' Aria shouts.

Dad doesn't change course. 'Hold on,' he shouts, bringing the boat even closer to the wind. The *Alcina* heels over steeply to the side.

The gears pound relentlessly, like a drumbeat marking progress. My body tenses as I urge the boat onwards. With millimetres to spare, the *Alcina* glides into the open sea and the gates slam closed behind us.

Workers line the shore, shaking their fists at us and cursing. I don't envy whoever must report back to Sir Waldred that we escaped.

It's not over though. A jet-ship appears on the horizon.

Aria tugs at my sleeve, 'Finn, save us! Use your powers.'

I close my eyes and let the image of a grey mist form in my mind. I stretch out my arms, my palms face down towards the sea, and slowly draw them upwards above my head.

'Yes,' Aria cries.

I open my eyes. Thick mist surrounds the boat, cloaking us from prying eyes. I stick out my tongue and taste it; it's salty.

Protected by the mist, we sail on. The roar of the jet-ship engines gets louder. We freeze to the spot. *Will they spot us?* Then starts to fade. They missed us by metres. We glide on in silence.

Now and then I hear voices from other boats, lost in the mist. Then they too fade into the distance as we slip silently past.

∽∾∽∾∽∾

Boats become less frequent as we travel further north. The air gets colder, and the wind gets sharper. I let the mist evaporate although we keep a constant watch for the trackers. The sea darkens to a hard steel-grey colour, just like in my vision. We pull on our furs for warmth, hugging them close. The icy wind claws at us, cutting right to the bone. Isolda lends Lisana a thick black bearskin coat. It hangs down to the ground, covering her bare feet.

I listen to the sea life. There are no dolphins this far north, just strange, rough sea creatures. Even the fish seem tougher, fiercer. I can't understand them; it's like they're speaking a foreign language.

The days pass slowly. Hour after hour, I sit in the crow's nest, keeping watch for the trackers. My breath comes out in icy smoke rings.

Early one morning, just as the first rays of sunlight crack the sky, I spot someone creep onto deck. I blink, squinting in the half-light, trying to see. It's Aria. *What is she doing so secretively?*

She tucks herself into a corner at the stern of the boat, hidden from the others, but not from my perch at the top of the mast.

I watch as she clasps her hands together then draws them apart. She pauses for a moment, then pretends to throw something into sea. Over and over again.

I slide down one of the ropes and dangle silently a few metres above her head. From here I can see more clearly. Between her hands there's a faint shape. For a moment, as she pulls her hands apart, it expands to fill the space. But then, just before she throws it into the sea, it disappears.

The wind catches me and I spin on the rope. I reach out and grab the mast with one of my hands to steady myself. A coin tumbles from my pocket. As if in slow motion, I watch it turning through the air. It lands on the deck with a small *plunk*. Aria spins round.

'Finn, what are you doing hanging off that rope?' she asks. 'Are you *spying* on me?'

I jump down onto the deck.

'No. I mean, yes. But what on earth are you doing?'

'None of your business,' she says, turning as red as a beetroot.

'I know what you're doing,' I say. 'You're practising your Air-Rider skills. Show me what you can do.'

'No, I'm not ready,' she says. 'It doesn't work.'

'Well, I saw most of it anyway, so you might as well,' I say.

Aria stands up in front of me and clasps her hands again. As she draws them apart, I realise the shape between them is moving. It's a tiny whirlwind. My jaw drops. 'That's so cool,' I say.

'Thanks, but I can't sustain it for long. Look,' she says, opening her hands. With a puff of wind, it dissolves. 'It's hopeless, I keep practising and practising but I just can't do it.'

'Have you been coming up on deck this early every morning and practising?' I ask.

'Yes. Ever since we left New London. The blood-magic feels stronger. I thought I was ready, but I can't control it. You can create tidal waves and sea-mists, and Pippin told me how you escaped through that flooded tunnel.'

'But you made the wind that knocked the bikers off the cliff?'

'I know, but that just happened. I didn't do it on purpose. I want to learn how to control my powers.

How to use them properly so I can impress Mum and Dad, and you.'

'Aria, you don't need to impress us. You're amazing. You're kind and clever and strong. You're just not old enough to use your powers properly yet. Look at me. I haven't even started my training yet and I'm older than you. At least you've started.'

'Thanks,' she says. 'Dad says you'll find a teacher at the castle.'

'That's what the stall-keeper in Izmarli said when I bought the pirrfu charm. How did he know?'

'I don't know, but I'd like to see that stall again. He might have a hyrshu air-charm,' Aria says. 'Then I'd feel like I was ready to become an Air-Rider.'

'I have a feeling you will find one anyway,' I say, wrapping my arm around her. 'Or it will find you.'

'Thanks. I'd like to be alone for a bit, please.' She turns her back on me and resumes her practice.

That evening, we sit on deck, wrapped in our furs, clutching mugs of steaming hot cocoa. Isolda tells us how she and Morgan hid the relic on Izmarli together many years ago to protect it from Sir Waldred.

'After you were born, Finn,' she says, 'everything changed. The elders wouldn't let her see you. Over the years, her hatred for the elders festered and grew.

She came to see the relic as a tool to punish them.'

'So why didn't she take it? She knew where it was, after all you put it there together.'

'She tried. She went back to get it, but there'd been an earthquake and the cave had changed. New cracks and crevices had formed. It wasn't where we left it. She accused me of stealing it, but I didn't.'

I recall the deep hollow the relic had been in, how it was wedged awkwardly into a corner.

'So that's why Sir Waldred couldn't find it, even with Morgan's map. It wasn't in quite the right place,' I say.

'Yes, but that's also why, when Sir Waldred learnt about you, he knew it would call to you as a blood-magic born Sea-Tamer, and it didn't matter if the map wasn't accurate. He *had* to get you to find it. He took me hostage to force Ragnar to get it, and to take you with him. Ragnar would never have agreed otherwise.'

'I knew it was all connected,' I say. 'But Sir Waldred knows about me now, I'm not a secret. Why does Morgan still want to punish the elders? Why doesn't she come to find me?'

'The years have hardened her soul. I think she's lost herself in the bitterness.'

'Then I'll find her, I'll stop her feeling lost. She doesn't mean to be bad; she's just sad.'

'Finn, that may be the truest thing you ever said.

The Morgan I knew as a girl wasn't a bad person. That little girl is still inside there somewhere. I hope you can find her.' Isolda hugs me tight, and a solitary tear splashes onto the ground.

Each mile crossed off on the chart is a hard-won achievement.

We line up on deck as we approach the Island of Gylen. Battered by the sea, it's a barren, ugly, brown lump of rock. A few brave trees hunch over against the wind, clinging onto life in this harsh environment. It's immediately recognisable as the place in my vision.

Rising out of the rocky cliffs is the castle. The solid grey granite walls soar above us. Even in ruins, it oozes power. I shudder to think how terrifying it must have been to approach as an invading army in days gone by.

Six stone turrets still mark the corners of the castle, the irregular shape following the outline of the cliff. There are no windows, just hundreds of narrow slits for the archers, pointing in every direction. Stone funnels overhang the battlements, ready to pour boiling tar down on anyone who tries to attack the castle from the sea. This was a castle built for war, not for princesses.

Near the shore, Aria grabs her bow and arrow, poised for an attack. But we land without seeing a single soul. The emptiness of the beach echoes. Only the wind comes to greet us, filling our ears with its chilly breath.

'Where do we go now?' Aria asks.

'Up there.' I point at the castle.

Dad leads the way as we scramble up the rough path. The castle looms above us, growing larger and larger as we climb.

'I don't like it here. It's creepy. Other than the wind, it's too quiet. Not a soul, not a single bird. I haven't even seen a seagull, and they get everywhere, like rats.' Aria grimaces, her long white hair whipping around her face in the wind. She pulls the collar on her coat further up and hunches her shoulders, shivering.

A heavy portcullis blocks the entrance to the castle. Thick iron bars flaked with rust suggest it hasn't been opened in years. Beyond the portcullis, under the archway, there's a vast wooden door, studded with iron spikes, and firmly closed. Visitors are clearly not welcome.

From the shadows steps a figure. Sir Waldred. My heart sinks.

'How did you know where to find us?' I ask.

'You are not the only one who knows how to find the elders,' he sneers.

'Although you are here, you still can't get in,' Lisana says. 'You need a guardian to unseal the gate for you.'

Lisana and Sir Waldred eye each other up like two champion boxers preparing for a fight.

'A small matter,' he says. 'Since you are here, we both know you'll do what I want.'

'In your dreams,' she scoffs. 'I'll never fall for your tricks again.'

'Have it your way, then.' Sir Waldred raises his hands. The earth starts to shake, great clouds of dust rise from the soil. I watch in horror. A huge explosion rips the ground apart. Stranded, Aria is cut off from us by the chasm in the ground.

'Aria, we can't get to you!' I cry.

I try to use my magic to pull the sea up the cliff, but it's too far and the wave breaks.

Hands behind her back, I watch Aria shape a whirlwind. She flings it towards Sir Waldred. Instead of disappearing as I feared, the whirlwind expands. He staggers back from the unexpected attack.

Oblivious, Aria presses forward, casting another, and another blast. She can do it! All the practice was worthwhile. My heart bursts with pride at my little sister.

Sir Waldred shrinks into the ground. Seconds later he reappears next to Dad, hitting him with a powerful blast of energy and sending him flying through the air. Dad smashes against a rock and crumples to the ground.

Aria casts a small whirlwind under her feet and rises up into the air, all the time continuing to hit Sir Waldred with her energy bombs.

Isolda joins in.

Water splashes in the cracked earth. I tug at it but it doesn't flow to me. I try again and finally, with an enormous heave, it erupts like a volcano. I throw the jet of water at Sir Waldred. He grabs Lisana and uses her as a shield.

Sir Waldred stamps his foot and a wall of rock shoots up behind him.

Lisana struggles free leaving Sir Waldred without a hostage. Exposed.

'Aria,' I yell. 'Together.'

Aria attacks him from above. I hit him with a geyser of water. Sir Waldred tries to block and dodge.

'Lisana, now. He's tiring,' I shout.

Lisana lifts her hands to attack his mind. Sir Waldred's eyes start to glaze over. Distracted by our combined assaults, his defences are low and she gets inside. But then he shakes his head, and his eyes are clear and cruel.

He claps his hands together. With a boom, he vanishes leaving just a cloud of dust and a deep crevasse in the ground.

We stare into the bottomless crevasse.

'Did he disappear into that?' I ask.

'Yes. He's gone, for now,' Lisana says. 'But he'll try again another day.'

'Well done, Aria,' Dad says. 'You're definitely ready for the next stage in your training.'

Aria beams. 'Thanks,' she says, blushing.

'When did you learn how to do that?' I ask.

'I wasn't sure I could. I've never managed before, but then I felt the power running through my veins,' she says. 'And I knew exactly what I needed to do.'

'Let's get inside this castle. It's time we met the

elders,' Lisana says, stretching out her arms. The thick bear-skin coat floats around her, billowing in the wild wind as if it were made of gossamer. She looks strangely regal. She starts chanting in a language that I don't know but seems vaguely familiar. After a while, a faint voice joins her. Then another, and another, until we have an unseen choir. The song rises and falls like a butterfly.

As the singing grows louder and clearer, I watch the iron portcullis start to move. It grinds its way upwards, pulled by some unseen power. Chunks of rust flake off as hinges, which must once have been well oiled, are forced into motion. Once it clears our heads, it clanks to a juddering halt. My feet do not want to budge, but inch-by-inch, I push myself forward. The others follow.

Crash. Behind us, the portcullis slams down. In front of us, the studded wooden door blocks the way. We're trapped.

SEVENTEEN

ELDERS

'I thought the elders wanted to meet us? What do we do now?' Aria says, pushing on the door. It doesn't budge. 'Should we knock or something?'

Lisana stops chanting and snaps out of her trance, her eyes refocusing. 'We wait,' she says.

After a few minutes, the wooden door creaks open a fraction. I hesitate. It's just wide enough for us to slip through, but do we really want to go inside? I look back. The portcullis is still firmly there; unyielding and unpassable. Do we have a choice? We can't go back. The only way is forward. Aria grips Mum's hand and, one-by-one, we cautiously edge past the door and step inside the castle.

As my eyes get used to the darkness, I see we're in a great hall. A massive fireplace is hewn into the stone wall at the far end of the hall, but it's empty. There is no comforting flicker and crackle from a log fire to warm this room. Faded tapestries hang limply from the cold, grey, stone walls telling long-forgotten tales. Shields and swords cover every other inch of wall

space. Slashes and gashes indicate these swords and shields are very far from being decorative items, they are weapons that have seen battles and blood. Each shield is painted with a different coat of arms. I look at them, searching for one with a white cross on a blue background, the black pearl with dolphin fins on the sides. Yes, it's there. I don't know whether to be relieved or worried.

A dark wooden table sits in the middle of the hall, the polish giving it a soft sheen despite the gloom. Twelve tall wooden chairs are pulled around it, their upright backs intricately carved, the brown leather seats brittle and cracked with age.

Nine figures start to form on the seats around the table, shadowy and insubstantial at first, but becoming more solid. Three of the seats remain empty.

'Excellent,' Lisana says, looking around the table. 'Now we have a proper gathering.'

A single voice echoes around the room. 'Welcome. We have been expecting you. Have you brought the relic?'

'Yes, he has it.' Lisana says, nudging me forward.

I stumble. *Am I doing the right thing? Should I trust these strangers?* I glance at Aria. It's as much her decision as mine. She nods. Reassured, I pull out the stone cube.

Aria unclasps a chain from around her neck and hands me the tiny key. I unlock the compartment where the pearl is safely nestled and lift it out. I haven't touched it since the vision and am prepared for another image to smash into my head, but nothing. It's strangely silent.

Three of the people around the table stand up and walk over to us. They must be the Sea-Tamer elders. One after another, they examine the pearl, the smooth surface contrasting with their gnarled hands. Their lips move but I hear no words. The air grows thick and heavy. They turn back to the table.

'Is it true? Is it time?' the other elders ask.

'Yes. There is no doubt. The relic is genuine. It is time.'

'Then do it.'

They walk to a cabinet in the corner of the room.

The first elder, a tall, thin, serious looking man with wiry grey hair opens a drawer. He reaches inside and pulls out a large clam shell. Cupping the shell in his hands, his arms outstretched, he waits.

The second elder, a delicate lady with fine oriental features and a kind smile, picks up a large marble urn. It looks far too heavy for such a tiny person to lift, but she shows no strain. She pours a thin stream of water into the shell. The room echoes as a few droplets splash onto the cold stone floor.

The third elder, a younger man with unkempt curly brown hair and a mischievous sparkle in his eyes, places the pearl in the shell. The water instantly fizzes and bubbles, multi-coloured puffs of steam rise from the shell. After a few minutes, the fizzing subsides.

The three elders turn to the rest of the gathering.

'It's done,' they say.

The thin elder lifts the pearl out of the clam shell. It's still beautiful, but it no longer shimmers. The flickering images have vanished. The magic is gone, it's just a pearl. They drop it back into the little compartment in the cube and close the lid. The lock dissolves, leaving no trace that the compartment ever opened.

'So, what happens to the relic now?' I ask.

'It has served its purpose.'

The elders hand the cube back to Aria. 'You'll be needing this,' they say.

Aria opens her mouth to speak, but the thin elder raises a bony hand to silence her.

The sea clan elders turn to Lisana. 'You are freed from your obligations as guardian of our relic. Thank you for your service. You may return to your old life.'

One after another, they swirl their fingertips through the water in the clam shell. Faster and faster they spin the water. A miniature whirlpool forms, like when you pull the plug out of a sink.

'Now,' announces the thin elder, lifting his hand from the shell. Lisana vanishes.

The room feels emptier without her presence.

'What?' I exclaim. 'Where's she gone? Where's Lisana? What have you done to her?' The force of my voice surprises me.

'Fear not. She's safe. She has returned to her family. Her life will continue as if she had never been a guardian.'

'That's good, right?' Aria asks. 'That's what she wanted, isn't it? To be home?'

'Indeed,' the elders say.

'But how can she have gone back to her family?' Aria continues. 'She said she was 400 years old. They must all be long dead?'

'Yes and no. Yes, in this time, you are right. They are all dead. But time is more flexible than you might think. It can be manipulated.'

'I never got to say bye to her,' I say. 'But I'm glad she's been forgiven for losing the relic. It wasn't her fault. And it could have been worse. Sir Waldred would have stolen it, if Mum and Morgan hadn't managed to hide it first. And she did try very hard to fix things.'

The air starts to crackle like static electricity. A shiver runs down my spine.

A flicker of movement catches my eye. The wooden carvings on the back of the chair in front of me start to bend and flex.

I glance around the table.

One, two, three, four.

Carvings on four of the chairs move as if they were alive. I rub my eyes and check again.

On one, I see a woman paddle a bamboo raft down a swollen river. Another shows a couple stroll barefoot along a beach, holding hands. Next, a fisherman casts his net from a rowing boat. Lastly, a small child pulls a bucket of water from a well and balances it on his head.

I stare at the other chairs. Nothing. They're solid, carved wood.

I nudge Aria and point at the moving images, but she has already seen them, her mouth opening and closing as she gawps in amazement.

'What happened to those chairs?' I exclaim, pointing at the carvings. 'How come they're moving? They're wooden. Wooden carvings. Carvings don't move.'

The tall, thin man snorts.

'Oh, just ignore him,' the petite woman says, tutting at the man. 'They're screens, monitors. Whatever you want to call them.'

'Like live TV?' I ask.

'Exactly. What you are watching is real. It's happening now, somewhere in the world. The screens monitor all those with clan powers. My one,' she says, pointing to her chair, 'shows all the Sea-Tamers in Asia.' Her face glows with pride.

'But why are only some working?' Aria asks.

'It only works for the Sea-Tamers. Their powers are free now,' I guess.

'Exactly. Once the powers were hidden in the relics, there were no signals for the screens to monitor. The carvings you see on those chairs,' she points around the room, 'are simply the last images, frozen in time.'

'Does that mean you'll be able to see me from now on?' I ask.

'Yes. Wherever you are, I will be watching you,' says the tall thin elder, his eyes narrowing.

But what if I don't want to be watched?

The three elders return to the table and take their seats.

Dad steps forward. He hasn't said a word since we entered the castle. He pulls me aside. 'Finn, that man,' he points at the third elder, 'is Kallan.'

The likeness is unmistakable. I see my reflection in his dark, curly hair and sun-tanned skin. A stark contrast to the gleaming white hair and pale complexions of Mum, Dad and Aria.

Kallan walks towards me and rests his hand on my shoulder. Such intimacy from a stranger, even if he is my birth father, is uncomfortable and I step back into Dad's protective arms.

'Hello Finn,' Kallan says, tears welling up in his eyes. 'It's OK, I understand. I can't believe it. I never thought I would see you again. Leaving you was the hardest thing we've ever had to do, but we had to keep you safe.'

He turns to Mum and Dad, embracing them as old friends. 'Thank you, Ragnar and Isolda, from the very bottom of my heart for looking after Finn these past twelve years.'

EIGHTEEN

PROPHECY

One of the elders who has not yet spoken beckons to Aria. She perches on the edge of her seat as if ready to take flight. 'As you know, the other clan powers are still sealed in their relics. They have not been freed. Only the Sea-Tamer powers were in the pearl.'

'But that's not fair,' Aria exclaims. 'The other clans need to be freed too.'

'I'm glad you feel like that,' says the bird-like elder. 'For I believe you can help.'

'I'll try,' Aria says bravely, although her voice quivers.

'There is a seat for you at this table, Aria,' continues the bird-like elder. 'But you must earn it. You must find the Air-Rider relic and free their powers.' She glances at the thin elder, 'But it will be your choice if you want to take your seat at the table. I will not force you.'

The bird-like elder offers Aria a leather-bound journal, tied up with string. 'This belonged to their guardian. It may be of assistance in your quest.' She lowers her voice to a whisper, 'Your quest is for a glass feather.'

'Silence,' one of the elders screeches. 'You know the conditions. It's not for us to decide if the time is right. The relic itself must decide if it wants to be found. We cannot help the Relic Hunters.'

'Why doesn't the Air-Rider guardian have the relic?' Aria asks.

'Sir Waldred killed him.'

'Oh no,' Aria says, clutching at a chair to steady herself. 'So why didn't Sir Waldred steal the relic when he killed the guardian?'

'The Guardian foresaw his own death and cast a powerful charm to protect it. You must follow the trail.'

'Aria, you can find it,' I blurt out. 'The relic will call to you, like the pearl called to me.'

'But I'm not twelve. I don't have my full powers yet.'

'You have enough,' the elder says. 'When you get close, the relic will make them much, much stronger. And what you lack in experience, you make up for in determination.'

'I don't even know where to start,' she says.

'With the journal?' I suggest. 'And I'll help you. You won't be on your own.'

'You can't leave,' the thin elder says, grabbing my arm. 'This place is yours.' He gestures to the empty chair next to him. 'You earned it.'

'But I didn't earn it,' I protest.

'You brought the pearl here,' the thin elder adds.

'Yes, but I didn't do it on my own,' I explain. 'I had lots of help.' I wave my arm in the direction of my family.

'And now you must help us,' the thin elder continues, his voice as sour as lemon juice. 'You must fulfil your obligations to the clan.'

'I can't,' I say, turning to Kallan, 'I'm glad I found you, but you can't expect me just to walk away from my family.'

'You should listen to him,' Dad says. 'I know it's hard, and there's a lot to take in, but the clan is important. Everything that Kallan and Morgan sacrificed was for the good of the clan.'

'There are other things that are important too. Like helping Aria. Like finding Morgan, before it's too late. You said you'd help me do that.'

'You need to decide what the right thing to do is, Finn. I can't decide for you,' Dad says.

The thin elder crosses his arms and glares at me.

I turn to the elders. 'I'm sorry. I can't stay here. I have to help my sister on her quest.'

'Sea-Tamer, I had hoped for so much … more … from you,' sneers the thin elder.

'What could be more important than finding the relics?' I ask.

'You must be trained,' he says. 'You must return one day.'

The group starts to fade back into the darkness.

'Wait,' I cry. 'Do you know where Morgan is?'

Kallan's voice replies, although what remains of his body is a mere shimmer. 'She also seeks the relics, but not for the clans. To give to Sir Waldred. You must find the relics before she does.'

With that, he dissolves entirely. We're alone. My question is answered though; I now know, without a shadow of doubt, whose side Morgan is on, and it's not ours. My heart sinks. I had hoped Sir Waldred was just trying to make me angry when he said Morgan worked for him, I had hoped it wasn't true. *Am I too late to save her?*

Lying on the table, in front of where the bird-like elder sat just a few moments before, is something shiny. A symbol. Puffs of wind curl together into a familiar shape: it's a hyrshu air-charm. I nudge Aria and point at it.

'I told you it would find you,' I say.

She picks it up and strokes it as if it was a kitten, drawn to it as I am to my pirrfu charm. 'I really am an Air-Rider now,' she murmurs.

'You always were,' I say. 'You don't need a charm to prove it.'

'Thanks. So what now?' Aria asks.

'We have to find the relic before Morgan.'

'But I don't know where to start looking. They didn't give us any directions,' Aria says, clenching her fists.

'The journal?' I suggest. 'What's in it? Maybe there's a clue.'

Aria opens it, her brows knit in concentration.

'What does it say?' I ask.

She reads aloud.

Where white eagles soar and no man can walk,
Above the clouds, yet still on the ground,
Lies the secret of which Air-people talk.
The winged girl must raise her clan around,
When the moon is cold and the stars point true,
For the time has come to start our world anew.

'Well that's not much of a clue is it,' I say, shoving my hands into my pockets, dejected.

'I think I understand it,' Aria says. 'Or at least some of it. The cold moon is the last full moon of the year. That's very soon.'

'And?'

'We need to get to an observatory before then to look at the stars, like the verse says.'

'There's the Royal Observatory in Greenwich, but I don't like the idea of going back to New London.'

'I know where we can go,' Pippin says. 'Spitbank Fort. It's an old army stronghold in the middle of the sea. It's off the south coast of England. Not too far from Portsmouth.'

'Why there?' Aria asks.

'Sir Waldred used it as a base, but it's empty now. We won't be seen … and there's a massive telescope.'

'Then that seems as good a place to start as any.'

THE END

OR IS IT JUST THE BEGINNING?

Reviews

If you enjoyed this book, please do tell your friends. It would be great if you could also leave a review wherever you buy books. Reviews help other readers choose their next book.

As well as online bookstores, there are many fabulous bookish websites, like Goodreads (www.goodreads.com) and Toppsta (www.toppsta.com), where you can leave reviews.

Ask a grown up to help if you aren't sure how.

Thanks very much.

Lexi

ACKNOWLEDGEMENTS

So many people have helped bring this from a few random ideas thrown about whilst sailing into a book, and I'm eternally grateful to you all.

Special thanks to Finlay, my son, for the constant support and encouragement, countless hours discussing the story, fight scenes (apparently I can't write a fight scene for toffee) and many of the illustrations. And to my husband for understanding, especially while I spent months in my editing cave.

I'm very lucky to have a fab team of beta readers. I'd particularly like to thank Theo, Raffi, and Lucy for the detailed feedback. Everything you suggested should be in here because it was all useful.

I couldn't have got to this stage without my patient, and picky, editors; Brian Keaney, Gary Smailes and Emma Mitchell. I've learnt so much from each of you during the journey, and look forward to working with you all again.

Author buddies, your encouragement, advice and support has been invaluable through the emotional roller-coaster of taking a first draft right the way to publication. Too many to mention you all, but you know who you are.

And finally, I'm a member of several fantastic book clubs. I would happily recommend two on Facebook: The Fiction Cafe and The Book Club (TBC).

Thanks again,

Lexi

ABOUT THE AUTHOR

Lexi Rees was born in Edinburgh and grew up in the Scottish Highlands. She now splits her time between London and Chichester, but still goes back to Scotland regularly.

She sails and rides horses, both of which she does spectacularly badly.

Eternal Seas was written whilst cruising in the Mediterranean; the storm described in the book was frighteningly real.

Concentrating on not falling off makes writing tricky whilst horse riding. It is definitely not recommended.

Resources

There are additional materials on the website, www. lexirees.co.uk.

Get in touch

If you have any questions, you can contact Lexi via the website (www.lexirees.co.uk) or social media.

Happy reading!